SHIVERS!

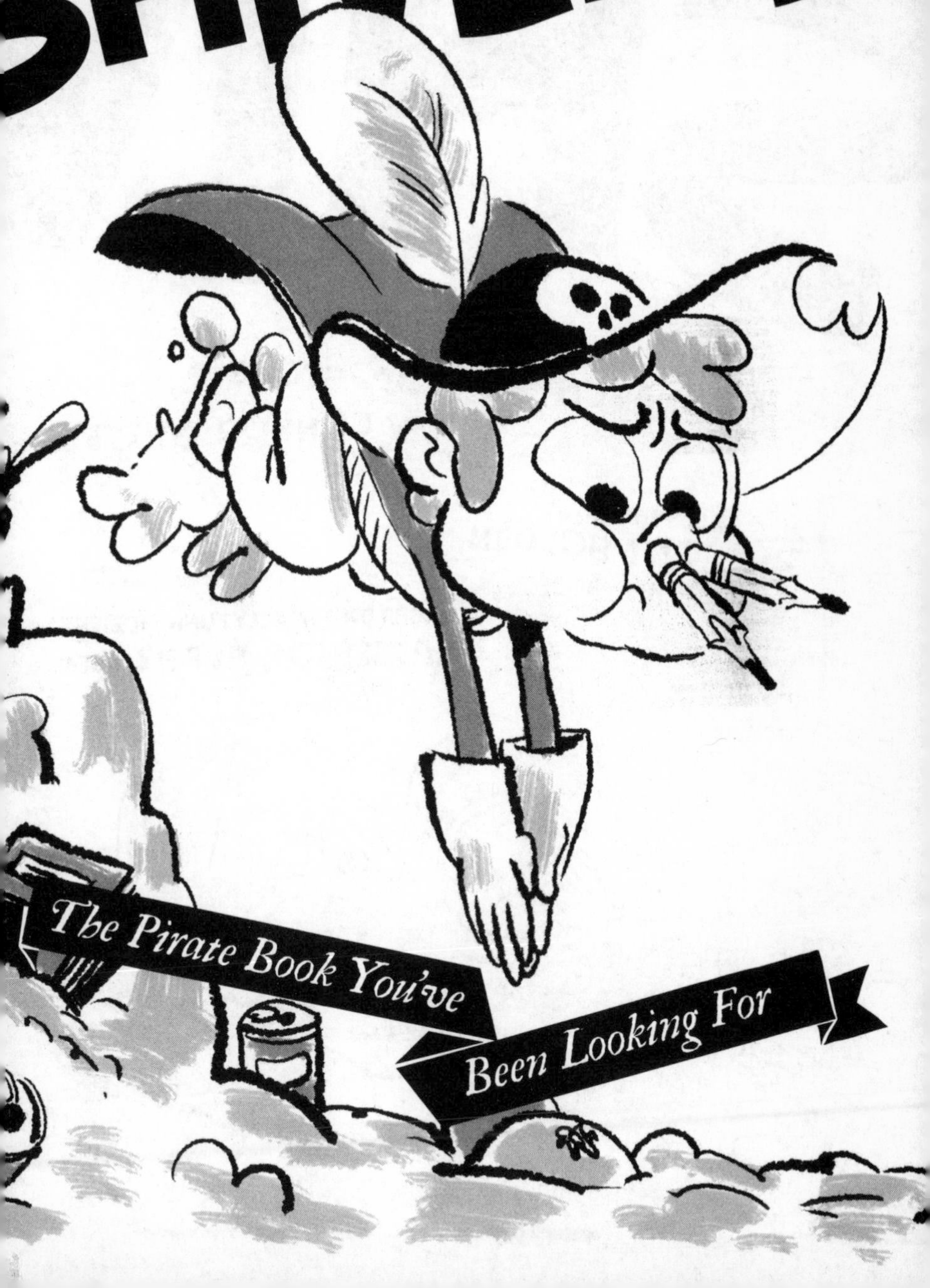

SHIV

BY **ANNABETH BONDOR-STONE**
AND **CONNOR WHITE**

ILLUSTRATED BY
ANTHONY HOLDEN

BASED ON A REALLY FUNNY IDEA BY
HARRISON BLANZ, AGE 9

ERS!

The Pirate Book You've Been Looking For

HARPER

An Imprint of HarperCollinsPublishers

MORE LAND

NYC

NEW JERSEY ELEMENTARY

?!!

WATER

For Jake and Sam

Shivers!: The Pirate Book You've Been Looking For
Text copyright © 2019 by
Annabeth Bondor-Stone and Connor White
Illustrations copyright © 2019 by Anthony Holden
All rights reserved. Printed in the United States of America.
No part of this book may be used or reproduced in any manner whatsoever
without written permission except in the case of brief quotations embodied
in critical articles and reviews. For information address HarperCollins
Children's Books, a division of HarperCollins Publishers, 195 Broadway,
New York, NY 10007.
www.harpercollinschildrens.com

Library of Congress Control Number: 2016952960
ISBN 978-0-06-231391-1

Typography by Joe Merkel and Erica De Chavez
18 19 20 21 22 CG/LSCH 10 9 8 7 6 5 4 3 2 1
❖
First Edition

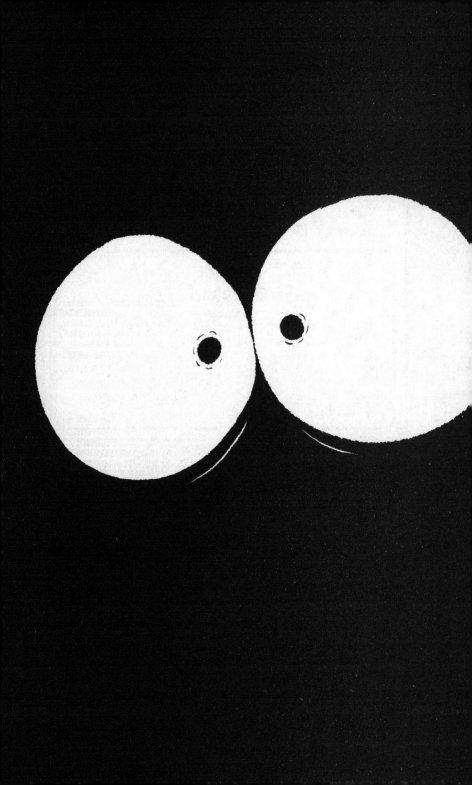

CHAPTER ONE

SUDDENLY, EVERYTHING WENT DARK.

Shivers the Pirate whirled around frantically, but all he could see was vast black nothingness. It was horrifying!

What is happening?! Shivers thought. Just moments ago, his parents had been standing beside him, but now they were gone. Everything was gone!

Did the lightbulbs break? Did the sun burn out? Did somebody steal my eyes?!

Panic bubbled up in his stomach like a stew left simmering too long on a stovetop. His whole body began to shake: his teeth were chattering, his arms were wiggling, the bunny slippers on his feet were doing a danger dance.

Where had all the light gone? Was he dreaming? Was he *nightmaring*? No, this had a for-real feel.

Shivers had spent his whole life trying to stay away from the dark, and now it was all he could see. He reached out in front of him, trying to find a light to turn on. But there was nothing there. His heart pounded in his chest so wildly it sounded like it was trying to tell a knock-knock joke.

There was only one thing he could do.

"AAAAAAAGH!" Shivers shrieked. He spun around in a circle then collapsed to the ground in a screap—which, if you don't already know, is a screaming heap.

Suddenly, all the light came flooding back. Shivers was lying in the sand on New Jersey Beach. His parents, Bob and Tilda, were standing above him. His mom was holding a bandanna in her hand.

"I told you the blindfold was a bad idea," said Bob, shaking his head.

"I thought it would make the surprise more fun," said Tilda.

"What surprise?" Shivers asked suspiciously. He hated anything unexpected and generally lived by the rule "Surprises cause demises."

"*This* surprise!" Tilda said, yanking him to his feet and turning him around. Towering right in front of him was a brand-new pirate ship. It was magnificent. The polished wooden hull shimmered in the sunlight. The crisp white sails fluttered majestically in the breeze. There was even a ring of floaties surrounding the deck.

"For me?!" Shivers asked.

Tilda nodded.

"My new ship!" he shouted with glee. "It's *finally* finished! I thought I'd *never* move back to my beautiful beach!" He picked up two handfuls of sand and kissed each of them. "It's been *years*!"

Really, it had only been three days, but Shivers had been so uneasy and so queasy that it felt like much longer. When his old ship, the *Land Lady*, had been destroyed, Shivers had been forced to move out to sea with his parents. Bob and Tilda had tried their best to make Shivers comfortable on their ship, but everything about it terrified him to the core. He wailed at every wave that rocked the ship and screamed at every seagull swooping by. Bob couldn't even toast the bread for a tuna melt without Shivers having a tuna meltdown. Shivers had a deep fear of toasters—they always pop up when you least expect it.

With all the screaming that had been going on, Bob and Tilda hadn't slept a wink. They knew they had to get Shivers out of the sea and back to the beach as fast as pirately possible. Luckily, Bob was an expert shipbuilder and Tilda was an expert at plundering all of Shivers's favorite things.

Shivers burst through the front door of the ship and squealed, "It's perfect!"

Bob and Tilda showed him all around the ship. His sleeping quarters were cozier than ever. He had brand-new curtains covered in pictures of kittens sitting in coffee cups. On top of his bed were hundreds of marshmallows sewn together to make the comfiest comforter imaginable. It also could come in handy as a midnight snack.

Shivers had just one question. "Where are the night-lights?"

"Where *aren't* the night-lights?" Tilda replied. She flicked a switch and the walls lit up with floor-to-ceiling night-lights, filling the entire room with a warm glow.

"Yes!" Shivers screamed. "Death to darkness!" He ran down the hall cheering. Which was a nice change, because usually he ran down the hall fearing.

In just a few short steps, he reached his brand-new kitchen. Waiting for him on the counter was his first mate, Albee.

"Albee!" Shivers cheered. "Can you believe this place?"

He looked around the kitchen, which was

customized for all his cravings. He flung open the fridge door and found it fully stocked with his favorite soft snacks, from jars of Jell-O to plates of pudding.

The pantry was packed with all kinds of mixes: brownie, pancake, and even trail. Albee had his own shelf, which was stacked with soft butter, his absolute favorite food.

Shivers placed Albee's bowl on the shelf so he could get a closer look. "This is all for you!"

"You'd butter not touch it!" Albee said. But sadly no one heard him because he's a fish.

Shivers marveled at the rest of the room. There was a giant microwave so he could make popcorn and heat up old pizza at the same time. The windowsill was decorated with pots full of daisies and sunflowers.

"We got you a flower bed," said Bob, beaming.

"Awww," said Shivers, "I'll have to get some flower pillows and a cozy flower blankie!"

Before Bob could explain what a flower bed

actually was, Shivers saw something very disturbing on the counter. "AAAGH! A toaster!" he screamed.

"Don't worry," Tilda said, putting her arm around him and walking him carefully toward the device. "It has slow-rise popping action. See?"

Two pieces of bread rose up slowly and silently from the toaster, like a sleepy jack-in-the-box.

Shivers's eyes popped open in amazement. "It's a *slow*-ster! I love it! It's *sooo* me!"

And with that, he hopped through the door and out to the main deck, twirling with excitement. Once he reached the deck, he kept on twirling.

"Hey, I could spin out here forever!" he exclaimed.

"That's what it's made for! It's a song and dance deck," said Tilda.

Shivers stopped short and gasped. The black surface of the deck was shiny and smooth. It stretched out in front of him for what looked like miles.

"Somebody jump on the piano! Key of G!" Shivers opened his mouth to sing.

Bob interrupted him. "Sorry, Shivers, we haven't gotten you a piano yet. But we did get you this!" He held up a rotting fish skeleton.

"It's a fishbone xylophone!" said Tilda proudly. "You play it with a wishbone!"

Bob demonstrated, clinking out a few flat notes.

Shivers leaped back in disgust. "Albee would be horrified! You're lucky he's busy eating butter right now."

Bob shrugged and threw the fish carcass off the deck; it landed on a beachgoer (who quickly became a home-goer).

Tilda smiled reassuringly. "I swear by all the squids in the sea, we'll get you that piano. But for now,

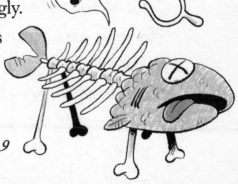

this will have to just be a dance deck."

Shivers sighed. "I guess I can live with that."

Tilda knew just the thing to cheer him up. "You haven't seen what's in here!" she said, walking across the deck. She opened the door to an enormous closet and Shivers could see that it was packed to the max with brand-new mops.

Shivers screamed in sheer delight. Next to singing and dancing, mopping was his favorite activity. He sprinted to the closet and grabbed as many mops as he could. He hugged them all, nuzzling his face into their soft fuzzy mop heads. "You know what they say–'Mop till you drop!'" Shivers picked up a bucket and tossed it to Tilda. "You get the water, I'll choose a mop, we'll meet back here in eight seconds!"

"No!" said Tilda and Bob at the same time.

"What? You need ten seconds?" Shivers asked.

"Shivers, you can't mop the deck today!" Bob barked.

"Why not?" Shivers was confused.

Bob's eyebrows furrowed into a stern scowl. His jawbone tightened with tension. Even his beard bristled nervously. He looked around cautiously, and then in a terrified whisper he uttered, "The Curse of Quincy Thomas the Pirate."

Shivers dropped all the mops. "The *what*? Of the *who*?"

Tilda mashed her lips with concern. She hated to tell Shivers about something so scary because he always got so screamy. But it had to be done. "If a pirate lets a single drop of water hit the deck on the day he gets a new ship, he'll be cursed by the ghost of Quincy Thomas the Pirate."

"Ghost?!" Shivers shrieked.

"Ghost?!" Bob bellowed, diving into the mop closet.

"Who said ghost?!" Tilda screeched, jumping in after Bob. Shivers followed close behind her and slammed the closet door.

"AAAAGGGHHH!!!"

They all stood in the dark closet screaming until Tilda shouted, "WAIT!" She clapped her hands over Shivers's and Bob's mouths. "Why are we in here screaming? There's no ghost on the ship. I was just telling you a tale about a ghost. A *grave* tale."

"Grave?!" Shivers screamed.

"Like the grave of a *ghost*?!" Bob wailed.

"GHOST!" Tilda hollered.

"AAAAAGGGGHHH!"

This happened seven more times.

Normally, Bob and Tilda would never get worked up into such a frantic frenzy. They were two of the bravest pirates at sea, you see, but any mention of ghosts sent them down a tunnel of terror. And it wasn't just them. *All* pirates had a boot-shaking, pantaloon-quaking, parrot-pooping fear of ghosts. That's the way it had always been and the way it would always be. It was the one thing that all pirates had in common with Shivers.

Finally Shivers and his parents managed to pull themselves together and push each other out of the closet. Tilda tucked her frayed hairs back into her bandanna. Bob un-bristled his beard.

"Let's pretend that never happened," he said. "Well, Shivers, I hope you liked the tour of your ship! We'd better get going. We've got some very important plundering to do with your brave brother, Brock."

"What about the curse?" Shivers asked.

"Don't worry," Tilda assured him. "Your ship is parked in the middle of the beach, about as far away from the water as a ship can get."

Bob turned to go but then stopped short. "We almost forgot! What's your new ship's name?"

Shivers wanted to give the ship a name that honored its best feature, which was the fact that it sat so safely and securely on the sand. "The *Groundhog*!" he announced proudly.

Bob and Tilda agreed it was the perfect name.

Shivers thanked his parents and waved as they sailed their own ship toward the horizon. He decided that now was the perfect time to test out his marshmallow comforter with a midmorning nap. As he went inside and closed the door, he didn't see the thick stack of angry gray storm clouds gathering above New Jersey Beach.

CHAPTER TWO

BOOM!!

Shivers sat up in bed with a start. He had been dreaming about growing his own pillows on a feather farm, but all that was gone now. He heard the sound again.

BOOM!

It was coming from outside. He ran to the porthole and saw just about the worst thing he could possibly see.

"CLOUDS!" he screamed. The smoke-black

rain clouds were swirling above Shivers's ship, and they were about to burst. If one raindrop spilled from those clouds and landed on his deck, he'd be cursed forever. There was only one thing to do: run around screaming like a crazy person.

Then, after that, there was only one *other* thing to do. "Protect the deck!" Shivers shouted, grabbing his comforter and scrambling outside. He spread it out as far as he could over the dance deck, but it hardly made a dent.

He dashed back into his sleeping quarters and ripped the kitten curtains off their rods. He dragged them out and laid them down next to the comforter. But it still wasn't enough.

BOOM!

More thunder rumbled from the sky. Shivers desperately wanted to cower in a closet next to a night-light, but he knew he had to get the *deck* covered before he could *duck* for cover.

He ran to the kitchen in search of more supplies. In one drawer he found a roll of plastic wrap, which he normally used to store leftovers. He also found some tinfoil, which he used to keep the plastic wrap company—it's dark inside the kitchen cabinets! Shivers stretched the foil and plastic wrap as far down the deck as they would go. But there was still one corner left uncovered.

Shivers spun around frantically, looking for something that might save him.

Shower curtain? he thought. But he only took baths.

Pancake platters? he wondered. *No, too precious.*

Then, an idea hit him like a spoonful of baby food.

"Bibs!" he cried. During his last adventure, bibs had become his most favorite fashion statement, and since then he had accumulated quite a collection. He sprinted to the hall closet, flicked on the night-light, and grabbed every bib he could see. Shivers ran back outside as the clouds cracked open. He flung the bibs like Frisbees and watched them land on the last uncovered corner just in time to catch the first drops of rain.

Shivers stumbled back into the kitchen and collapsed on the floor. He was proud of himself for covering the deck so quickly. He was glum about his new comforter getting soggy. And he was still disappointed that he wasn't *really* a pillow farmer. But most of all, he was very hungry.

He stood up to get a snack. When he opened the pantry door, he saw Albee still perched on his butter shelf.

"Albee! I forgot you were in here!" said Shivers, delighted.

The butter was gone and Albee looked very full. Shivers always wondered how Albee was able to get out of his bowl and eat entire sticks of butter when no one was watching. Then again, there were lots of things Shivers wondered about Albee.

Albee was so excited about all the butter in his belly that he was swimming around in sloppy, speedy circles.

Shivers reached out to grab the bowl, but at that moment, Albee careened into the glass. The bowl teetered on the edge of the shelf and crashed to the floor.

"My first mate!" Shivers screeched as he gathered Albee in his hands. He filled a ziplock bag with water, then dropped Albee inside and breathed a sigh of relief. But then he looked at the mess on the kitchen floor. Trickling out from under the broken bowl was a steady stream of water. Shivers watched in horror as it leaked through the doorway and out onto the deck.

He clutched Albee's bag tightly and held it up to his face. Shivers and Albee locked eyes, and Shivers screamed,

"I'M CURSED!!"

CHAPTER THREE

MARGO CLOMPS'N'STOMPS SAT IN the back of Mrs. Beezle's fifth-grade class and worked on her rubber-band ball. She was hoping that soon it would be so big that she could grab on to it and bounce right out of school. For now, it was about the size of a softball, so she had a long road ahead of her.

At the front of the room, Mrs. Beezle was going on and on about the geography of Antarctica. Margo was trying her best not to listen and had even stuck erasers in her ears to help (which Mrs. Beezle had told her again and again was not safe and not something to encourage in other kids and that some day those erasers might get stuck and never come out). Margo knew she would go to Antarctica someday, and she didn't want Mrs. Beezle giving away any surprises. All she could do now was hope that the rain trickling down the window would stop before recess.

She looked down at her brand-new bright-yellow watch. The second hand plodded along more slowly than a sleepy sloth on a stroll. Her dad had bought her the watch, insisting that she start coming home on time. But all it had done so far was dissect Mrs. Beezle's lessons into thousands of endless seconds.

When the morning announcements finally came on, Margo perked up and took the erasers out of her ears. She needed a break from the Beezle blabbing. Plus, she loved pretending that the sound com-ing from the speaker was actually a ghost haunting the class-room. Seriously, you should try it. It's awesome.

"Good morning, students!" said the crackling voice of the principal. "Hope you New Jersey Jaguars are having a roaring good morning!"

All the students rolled their eyes at the same time.

"Today, lunch will be ham in ham sauce. The chess club has officially been changed to the checkers club. And skateboarding will no lon-ger be allowed on the roof. I don't know why we thought that was a good idea. Now learn a lot and show off those spots! Go Jaguars!"

The speaker clicked off. Then suddenly, it clicked back on again.

"Oh, one more thing," the principal added. "Can someone please come to the front hallway and help the kid dressed as a pirate get his head unstuck from the stuffed jaguar's mouth? He won't stop screaming."

Margo gasped. The rubber-band ball dropped from her hand and landed with a THUD . . .

thud . . . thud. She only knew one person who dressed like a pirate and screamed all the time. And it was probably the same person who would get his head stuck in a fake jaguar's mouth. She had to get to Shivers right away. Luckily, the ball was bouncing all over the room, and it distracted Mrs. Beezle long enough for Margo to dart out the door.

Margo sprinted down the long beige hallway, following the sound of the screaming. When she got to the front entrance of the school, she saw two pantaloon-clad legs flailing from the mouth of Fluffy the Jaguar, the giant stuffed school mascot. She grabbed onto Shivers's ankles and pulled. He popped out and fell to the floor, wheezing

uncontrollably and clutching Albee's bag in his lap.

Margo helped him up and gave him a hug as big as the grin on her face. "Shivers! Albee! I'm so happy to see you! What are you doing here? And how did you get your head stuck in that jaguar?"

Shivers wiped some fuzz from his forehead. "Well, I've always been told that when you see a wild animal you should stick your head in its mouth to show it that you're not a threat."

"That's terrible advice," said Margo.

"That's what *I* said," Albee complained, but no one seemed to notice.

"Margo," Shivers said urgently, "I've got bigger problems than this jaguar security guard. I'm cursed!"

"You're what?" Margo asked.

"CURSED! I'm cursed by the ghost of Quincy Thomas the Pirate!"

"Who's that?"

"I don't know! Some evil old pirate!" He grabbed

Margo's shoulders and shook them. "You've got to help me get uncursed!"

Margo was thrilled. It had been three days since she had last hit the high seas with Shivers. School had been so boring that she was crawling out of her skin. And she hated crawling–it was for babies. Her brain started whirring with the excitement of pirate ghosts, evil curses, grizzly sword fights, bloodthirsty sea creatures, and–

"Margo! Are you going to help me or what?" Shivers shook her shoulders again. She had been standing there with a dreamy grin on her face for the last five minutes.

"Of course!" Margo said, leading Shivers into the school. As badly as Margo wanted to leave, she knew they had to make one stop first. "If we're going to get you uncursed, we need the facts. We're going to the library."

Shivers narrowed his eyes. "If we need facts, shouldn't we be going to the *truth*bary?"

Margo and Albee both sighed, and the three made their way down the hall.

"I've never been to a school before," Shivers marveled.

"I have," said Albee, but no one understood he was making a fish joke.

They passed by the gym and Shivers stopped to look inside. He saw a kid climbing a tall rope. "Where is he going?"

"Nowhere," Margo explained. "He just goes up and down as many times as he can."

"So he's a human yo-yo?" Shivers said with a shudder.

They kept walking. "This is the art room," Margo said, pointing to a classroom full of kids working with clay.

Shivers pressed his face to the window. "Wow, those sculptures of children are so realistic!"

"Those are real kids, Shivers." Margo shook her head in disbelief and yanked him down the hall by his sleeve.

They were nearing Mrs. Beezle's classroom, so Margo decided to pick up the pace. She hurried past the door, ducking down so that not even her ponytail would pop up in the window. Shivers lagged behind to peer in. He was spellbound—and they weren't even having a spelling test.

Mrs. Beezle was busy asking questions and half of the students were holding their hands high in the air. Shivers turned the doorknob to go inside.

"Shivers!" Margo whispered furiously. "What are you doing?"

"There's a whole bunch of kids in there who need high fives!" he explained.

"Come on! You're going to get us caught!" she said, pulling him away.

They turned a corner and reached a pair of wooden doors with a sign above them that said, WELCOME TO THE LIBRARY. NOW BE QUIET!

Margo pointed at the sign. "Can you do that, Shivers?"

"No problem, easy peasy!" Shivers said, walking

through the doors. "AAAAAGHH!" he screamed.
"It's a book graveyard!"

"Quiet!" chirped the librarian. She was a tiny
woman in an enormous sweater as frayed and
fluffy as her frizzy hair.

"Sorry." Shivers winced, retreating into one of
the many rows of bookshelves. He had never seen
so many books before. Books weren't very pop-
ular with pirates. Growing up, Shivers's parents

had only one book. It was a book of maps. He tried to read it once but someone had drawn an *X* on almost every page, which made it very hard to get through.

Shivers looked wide-eyed at the seemingly endless stack of stories. Then he grabbed the biggest, most colorful book in sight. "Oooh, this one is pretty! Maybe we can find something useful in here."

Margo looked over his shoulder. "Shivers, that's just a book of fairy tales."

"AAAAAAGHH!" Shivers screamed. "I didn't know fairies had tails! That's disgusting!"

The librarian whipped around the corner of the bookshelf. "Silence!"

"He's never been in a library before," Margo explained. "He doesn't understand the rules."

"Forget the rules, I'm just looking out for my extremely sensitive ears!" the librarian whined. "I hate loud noises! I have ever since I was a small child and my father played the jackhammer."

"The jackhammer's not a musical instrument," said Margo.

"Exactly," the librarian said, her shoulders slumped. "And I'm not even a real librarian, I just needed to work somewhere quiet." She turned on Shivers. "And you're ruining that! If this section is too scary for you, why don't you try a picture book?" She grabbed one from a nearby shelf and handed it to Shivers. But it wasn't just a picture book. It was a pop-up book.

Shivers opened it and the pictures practically pounced off the page. Shivers screamed, flinging the book wildly across the library.

The librarian shook her tiny fist in the air and screamed, "BE QUIET!!!" The volume of her own voice made her cringe and cover her ears with her hands. "My ears! My precious ears!" she cried softly, then ran to her desk, where she kept a jar of cotton balls to stuff in her ears in case of emergency.

Shivers shuddered. "I didn't realize libraries

were so dangerous."

Margo shook her head. "Before you, I didn't realize a lot of places were so dangerous. Come on, we're in the wrong section."

Margo, Shivers, and Albee snaked through the shelves until they reached the nonfiction section. Margo scanned the subjects. "Pilots, Pinwheels,

Piranhas . . . Pistachios? No, we've gone too far. Here we go. Pirates!"

Margo got up on tiptoe to check out the small

collection of books. A worn, leather-bound book caught her eye. Immediately, she knew it was the pirate book she'd been looking for. It was called *The Pirate Book You've Been Looking For.* As she pulled it off the shelf, Shivers and Albee admired the gold letters on the pale green cover.

The book was divided into three sections. "Pirate Heroes," Margo read, "Pirate Zeros, and Pirate Curses." She flipped to the last section and found the entry on Quincy Thomas the Pirate.

She began to read aloud, "Quincy Thomas the Pirate terrorized the Seven Seas with his blood-crusted sword and ugly face. One day, he attacked a pirate crew on their brand-new ship. He was about to brutally slaughter the entire crew when they began to cry. Their tears made a puddle on the deck. Quincy slipped on the puddle and fell to his death. Now, on the day a pirate gets a brand-new ship, if he lets a drop of water touch the deck, he'll be cursed by the ghost of Quincy Thomas."

When Margo looked up from reading, she

saw that Shivers and Albee were curled up in a ball on the floor. "That's the scariest story I've ever heard," Shivers stammered. "What happens when you're cursed?"

Margo read on, but decided it was probably not a good idea to read out loud anymore. As she read to herself, the color drained from her face. Finally she shut the book and turned to Shivers.

"Well, the good news is there is one way to break the curse. You have to plunder a piece of treasure and bring it to Quincy Thomas's grave on the Cape of Cods."

"That sounds like *bad* news," Shivers moaned. "What's the badder news?"

Margo bit her lip. "If you don't succeed, the ghost of Quincy Thomas will hunt you down and eat you before your next birthday."

Shivers's eyes popped with panic. "Margo," he said, "My next birthday is *tomorrow*."

Then he opened his mouth to scream louder than he had ever screamed in his whole life.

CHAPTER FOUR

BY THE TIME MARGO got Shivers to stop screaming, the librarian had quit her job and run off to work at a mime school. Margo scooped him up from his meltdown and hurried him out into the hallway with her eye toward the exit.

"What am I going to do? And how am I going to do it? I only have one day before I'm eaten by a ghost!" Shivers cried.

"You're not going to get eaten by a ghost. We just have to find some treasure and make our way to the Cape of Cods!" Margo said excitedly.

"How am I supposed to find treasure?" he groaned.

Margo was already two steps ahead of him. "Tie up a pirate crew and jab them with swords until gold falls from their pockets!"

"Did you say jab?!" Shivers squeaked, gnawing at his fingernails.

"Or we could swim into the belly of a man-eating whale and hope he ate someone who was carrying treasure!"

"Did you say swim?!" Shivers balked.

"Or we could load ourselves into a giant cannon, point it toward a dark cave, and then–"

"STOP!" Shivers screamed, mostly because he didn't want to hear the end of the idea but also because he had spotted something glimmering at the end of the hall. He ran toward it and skidded to a halt. "Look! There's treasure *right here*!"

He was staring up at the school's trophy case.

Shivers was overwhelmed with the options. There was a golden statue for first place in football, a silver goblet for second place in soccer, and a shiny plaque that said, *To the Chess Team—You should really consider checkers.*

Shivers grabbed the hinges of the glass doors and pried them open. He grabbed the first trophy in sight, but it was made of plastic. They were all made of plastic!

Then he heard the sharp shriek of a whistle,

followed by a voice barking, "You're busted, buster! Back away from the case!"

Shivers turned around and saw a skinny little stick of a kid huffing toward him, carrying a yellow notebook and wearing an orange sash.

Margo's big green eyes bulged like baked eggs. "The Hall Monitor!"

"The Hall Monitor?" Shivers backed away from the trophies with his hands held high. "What's that? Are we going to Hall Jail?!"

"No, but I will write you a yellow slip," said the Hall Monitor, holding his pen above the page threateningly.

"What does that do?" Shivers asked.

"No one knows!" said Margo. "Run!"

As Margo, Shivers, and Albee charged around the corner, they heard the Hall Monitor bellow, "It goes on your permanent record!"

They bounded into the front lobby, past the stuffed jaguar, and out the front doors. The rain had stopped, and the playground was packed with kindergartners running around wildly and screaming at the top of their lungs.

Shivers braced himself and looked around in fear. "Margo, what's going on? There must be an emergency! You save these kids; I'll run and hide. Albee, you supervise."

"It's just recess," Margo explained, shaking her head in disbelief.

"Is Recess the name of an angry bear?!" Shivers recoiled.

Before Margo even knew where to begin, a little girl in pink overalls ran up to Shivers and smacked him on the knee.

"You're It!" she shouted, and then ran away.

Shivers suddenly looked more uncomfortable than a cow doing a cartwheel. "I'm . . . It?" he said with utter confusion.

Margo could see that Shivers was nearing a gold-medal meltdown. She snatched Albee from his hands to protect him from any flailing.

Shivers began to pull at his hair. "What does that mean? What is It? What am I? HOW AM I IT?"'

"They're playing tag and you're It," Margo said.

"I'm not It, I'm Shivers! I'm a human boy!"

Margo threw up her hands in frustration and sighed. "Shivers, you don't get it."

"I have to *get* It?! I thought I *was* It!" Shivers clutched his cheeks. "Margo, if you don't start making sense, I'm going to throw an It fit!"

"All *It* means is that you're the one who's supposed to chase after everybody!"

"Ohhh." Shivers finally understood. "Well, that's a problem because I don't chase. I *get* chased."

The gaggle of kindergartners was staring at Shivers expectantly, ready to run.

"You'd better tag someone, otherwise they'll never let us get out of here. Kindergartners . . ." Margo shuddered. "They're not kind. And they don't garden."

Shivers took one lousy lunge toward them and they all leaped backward, screaming with delight. He gingerly followed a particularly slow blond boy onto the jungle gym. But just as Shivers had almost caught *up*, the boy decided to take the slide *down*. And there was no way Shivers was getting on that death trap.

Margo was starting to worry that they would waste their whole day here. She had already wasted enough of her day at school. If they were ever going to make it to the Cape of Cods, she was going to have to get Shivers out of the sandbox. There had to be a way to make these kids stand still.

But how? she thought.

Then, suddenly, the answer came in the form of a question.

"Hey!" Margo yelled as loud as she could. "Who here likes pepperoni pizza?!"

The kindergartners stopped in their tracks

and raised their hands high in the air. Shivers
saw opportunity knocking—well, more like
holding its hand up for a high five. He ran down
the line of kids, high-fiving each of them with a
satisfying smack.

The kindergartners were so confused. "Everyone is It!" they shouted as they chased each other in circles. Margo, Shivers, and Albee ran across the yard and out of the gate.

CHAPTER FIVE

SHIVERS AND MARGO SAT on the captain's deck of Shivers's new ship. He couldn't believe that he was already taking it out on a dangerous mission.

As the ship splashed over the surf, Shivers whined, "Margo, turn around and head back to the beach! This ship is called the *Groundhog*, not the *Waterhog*!"

"Which is scarier? Sailing on the open sea," Margo said as she held out one hand, "or getting eaten by an ugly pirate ghost on your birthday?" She held out the other hand.

"Is there a third hand?" Shivers asked hopefully.

Margo shook her head.

"Okay, point taken," Shivers said. Normally he hated taking anything pointy, but he had to admit Margo was right. So he did the only thing he could do at a time like this. He leaned over the railing and puked. "Now that that's over with, which way do we go?"

Margo pulled the pirate book out of her backpack and turned to the last page, which was a detailed map of the Eastern Seas. The Cape of Cods jutted into the sea, far north of New Jersey Beach. On the map, it looked like a bony finger beckoning them toward it.

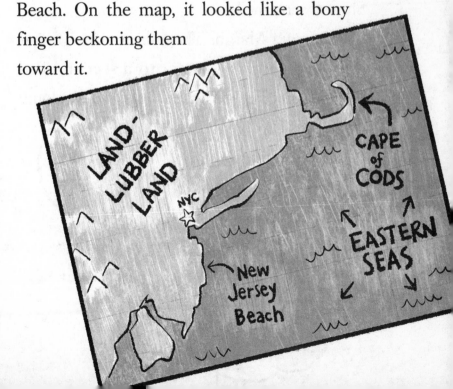

"*That's* where we're going?" Shivers said in disgust. "It's the ugliest cape I've ever seen. And I know capes."

"We can make it up there before the end of the day, but we're going to have to move fast," Margo said, spinning the helm to steer the ship north. "And we're going to have to be prepared." Margo flipped through the pirate book to the section on Quincy Thomas. She had to make sure they knew all the details. "Now, where was I? Oh right, the part where you die tomorrow."

Shivers screamed.

"Sorry," said Margo. Then she ran her finger down the page until she got to a section titled "So You Think You're Cursed?" She read it aloud:

"Here's a handy list of signs that you are one-hundred-percent definitely cursed by the ghost of Quincy Thomas the Pirate:

1. You will smell his foul odor everywhere you go.
2. You will start to become as violent and merciless as he was.
3. There is no 3. You'll be dead by then."

"AAAAGGH! Margo, why did you tell me that?!" Shivers wailed.

"It's better to know than to be in the dark," she said.

"Hm . . . I do hate the dark."

"Exactly! Now if we start to see any of those signs, we'll know the ghost is getting closer. And in the meantime, we have to plunder some treasure!" Margo said, pumping her fist in the air.

"Could you not sound so excited about it?" Shivers groaned.

Margo couldn't help it. She was overjoyed to be on a real pirate plundering mission. "Plundering treasure is as easy as pie."

Shivers narrowed his eyes. "Have you ever tried to actually make a pie? It's extremely difficult."

"Okay, then. It's a piece of cake!"

"Margo, you know I can't eat cake! I get *C*-sick!"

Margo couldn't stop herself from laughing. "Come on, let me teach you how to plunder." She climbed the ladder down to the song and dance deck, where they would have more room.

"Oh *this* is going to go well," said Albee.

But before Albee's bubbles reached the surface, Shivers scooped up Albee's bag in one hand and a bowl of popcorn he'd been munching on in the other. Then he followed gingerly behind Margo.

"There are all sorts of ways to plunder treasure," Margo began. "One is by force."

"What does that–"

Shivers never got a chance to finish his question

because Margo was already charging at him like an angry waterhog. She pried the popcorn bowl from his hands with such strength and speed that by the time he figured out what was going on, Margo was already on the other side of the deck, triumphantly throwing popcorn in the air like kernels of confetti.

"Hey, that was my after-school snack!" Shivers whined.

"You don't go to school," said Margo.

"I did *today*," he argued. "It was my first after-school snack ever."

Margo thought that plundering by force was not going to be Shivers's strong suit. She handed the bowl back to him. "Another way to plunder treasure is by threatening." She opened up the mop closet and scooped a skinny stack of mops under her arm. Then she pointed at Albee and in her most gravelly growl said, "Give me that fish or all these mops are going overboard."

"Not my mops! Here, take him! I don't even

know who that fish is!" Shivers tossed Albee's bag over to Margo.

Margo caught the bag. Albee was miffed.

"Just let the mops go!" Shivers pleaded. "What have they ever done to you—besides clean your floors until they sparkle?"

"Okay, okay!" Margo put the mops back and slammed the closet door. This kind of plundering wasn't going to work for Shivers, either. Luckily, she knew another way: distraction. She pointed above her head and said, "Shivers! Doesn't that cloud look like a cozy cup of hot cocoa?"

Shivers lay down on the deck and looked straight up at the sky. "Which cloud? Where?" he said excitedly.

"Never mind. It must have blown away," she said.

Shivers hopped back up to his feet and noticed that Margo had one hand behind her back.

"Shivers, where are your bunny slippers?" she asked, trying to contain an enormous grin.

Shivers carefully glanced down and saw his

bare feet on the deck. His bunny slippers were nowhere in sight.

Margo whipped the slippers out from behind her back. "Got 'em!"

But Shivers wasn't listening. He was still staring down in terror. He held out a shaking hand and pointed at his feet.

Then he cried out, "TOENAILS!" He leaped in the air, kicking wildly, trying to flick his feet right off his ankles. "Get away from me!" He sprinted across the deck, but it turns out feet are the hardest things to run away from. Then he squeezed Margo's shoulders and shouted, "They're following me!! There's no escape!"

Margo hadn't known Shivers would go into a toenail tizzy, and now she had to get him out of it. She tackled him on the deck, sat on him to keep him still, and popped the slippers back on his feet.

Shivers breathed a sigh of relief. "Well, that was just about the worst thing that ever happened. I haven't seen those toenails in days, and no matter how much beauty sleep they get in my bunny slippers, they just seem to get uglier."

"Why are you afraid of toenails?" Margo asked.

"The real question is why aren't *you*? They make my toes look like fingers. No matter how much I clip them away, they keep crawling back. And they're full of toe jam! Which does *not* taste good on toast, believe me."

"Ugh!" Margo recoiled.

"Plus, I have a rule. If Albee doesn't need something, neither do I."

"Tails over nails!" Albee said, waving his tail proudly.

"It's a good thing I panicked enough to get these slippers back on my feet." Shivers gasped and clapped his hands as he had a realization. "Hey! I took the slippers from you! Does that mean I plundered?"

Margo was impressed. "You did! In your own special way."

"I panic-plundered!" Shivers announced proudly. "Look at me! I'm the world's greatest plunderer!"

"I don't know if I'd go that far," Margo said warily.

At that moment, they heard the screeching squawks of several seagulls flying above their heads. They looked up and watched the gulls soar through the sky and land on a nearby ship. The ship was almost twice the size of the *Groundhog*. It didn't have a flag or a name, just a number written on its dark red hull. The deck was packed from front to back with shiny–

"Treasure!" Shivers said breathlessly. He ran to the captain's deck and spun the steering wheel all the way to the left, sending the *Groundhog* swirling toward the strange ship.

Margo excitedly readied herself at the anchor. As soon as they had pulled up close enough to the ship, she plunged the anchor into the water.

Shivers flew down the stairs from the captain's deck and said, "Let's plunder that treasure and get this ghost gone!"

The giant ship was moving through the water more slowly than a marmalade parade. As it drifted nearer, Margo scrunched up her nose. "Something smells fishy."

Shivers was too excited to listen. He grabbed on to the railing and jumped onboard, landing with a crunch.

Margo had no choice but to grab Albee and leap onto the ship, too.

There was a woman at the wheel wearing dingy overalls and a checkered hat with flaps over the ears. "Hey! What are you doing here?" she called down to them from the captain's deck.

Shivers planted his feet and raised his fist in the air. "We're here to plunder! Give us everything you've got!"

CHAPTER SIX

"SURE! NO PROBLEM!" THE captain said happily. Then she came down from the deck to help them.

Shivers looked at Albee with amazement. "See? I am the world's greatest plunderer," he said, making his way to the main deck.

Albee was skeptical. So was Margo. Plundering wasn't supposed to be this easy. In fact, nothing with Shivers was supposed to be this easy. She followed behind him suspiciously, then suddenly she heard him scream.

"AAAAAGGGHH!" Shivers was up to his knees in a greasy gray sludge. He was surrounded

by empty soda cans, ratty gym socks, and black-
ened banana peels. His eyes stretched out in
horror as he looked at the mountain of moldy
mysteries. "IT'S ALL TRASH!" he shouted,
pinching his nose.

"Of course it's all trash. This is a trash barge!"
said the captain. "Why else would I have these
nose plugs?" She popped two tiny rubber plugs
out of her nose and took a deep breath. "Yikes,"
she said, and popped them back in.

Fear mounted on Shivers's face. Margo could tell he was in a pre-panic that could erupt at any moment. "I can't believe we barged onto a trash barge!" he cried. "We're never going to find any treasure, and I'm going to get eaten by a ghost! Who will take care of Albee? He needs me to feed him fish flakes, to give him fresh water, to sing his favorite songs as loud as I can several times a night!"

"I've been meaning to talk to you about that last one," said Albee.

"Don't worry, Shivers," said Margo. She waded into the pile of garbage and rolled up her sleeves. "One man's trash is another man's treasure!"

"Little girl!" the captain said, squishing and squashing her way over to them. "If I were you, I wouldn't put my bare hands in there. It's full of dangerous things . . . like bear hands." She handed gloves to Margo and Shivers, then extended her own gloved hand. "I'm Shelly," she said with a smile. "But my friends call me Smelly."

"That's not very nice," said Margo.

"It certainly isn't," said Shelly, "But that's what I get for being in charge of a trash barge."

"We're trying to find . . ." Margo paused. It was hard to explain that they were searching for a present for an angry ghost. "Do you mind if we take a look around?"

"Sure! Make yourself at home," said Shelly. "But don't really. This is a terrible place to live."

Margo picked through the pile of debris, trying

desperately not to breathe in through her nose. At one point she saw a glint of silver, but it turned out to be a wad of tinfoil covered in fish oil. She picked up a string of pearls, only to find that it was really a string of spitballs. Then, she thought she'd found some gold coins, but they turned out to be chocolate coins *and* all the chocolate was gone, so the whole thing was a bust. "Maybe one man's trash is just another man's trash," she sighed.

"AAAAAAGGH!" Shivers wailed.

Margo looked up at him. She couldn't tell if this was a scream of panic or a scream of delight. "Did you find something?" she asked.

"No! My gloves are too tight!" he squealed. Shivers had just figured out how to put his gloves on.

Margo sighed. "Well, you can take them off now. There's no treasure here."

Shivers groaned. Taking the gloves off was going to be even harder than putting them on.

"We've got to go," said Margo. Then she looked around, confused. "Where's Albee?"

"I put him on this stinking pile of soggy socks,"
He trudged through the trash and gasped. "Oh no!
It's a *sinking* pile of soggy socks!" The sock mound
had caved in, and a cascade of crusty socks was
slipping toward the center. Albee was nowhere in
sight. Shivers was everywhere in fright.

He spun around in circles, stirring up the socks
so it looked like he was in a disgusting dryer.
"ALBEE!" he screamed. He found two short pencils, and despite his worry that they'd get stuck
forever, he bravely rammed them in his nose
(erasers first).

"I'm coming to get you, buddy!" he howled. Then he took a deep breath and dove in.

Margo marveled at Shivers. When his best friends were in trouble, he was able to put his fears behind him. Still, he could always turn around and his fears would be right there where he left them. She could only see his bunny slippers kicking above the surface as he clawed his way through the muck. She found two pieces of candy corn to use as nose plugs of her own and plunged in after him.

As soon as their heads smashed through the trash, Margo and Shivers were hit with a stew of sickening smells: sour cabbage and bitter beets . . . head sweat and slime-soaked meats . . . baby bathwater and used shoe juice . . . all simmering in the stale stench of unfresh-baked cookies. The pencils in Shivers's nose weren't doing much to erase the stink, and Margo's candy corn wasn't helping, either.

Shivers was trying to slog through a tangled

web of old street meats and moldy string cheese when he had to come up for air. But he didn't come up high enough and instead he wound up inhaling a mouthful of hair.

Margo came up, too, and yanked Shivers from the trash. He was spitting and sputtering and muttering all at the same time. "Albee's gone! He's *gone*! I thought I had found him but it was just an old orange!" Shivers held up a piece of rotting orange.

Then he fell to his knees and squeezed the fruit. As the juice ran down his arm, he shouted, "WHY?!"

"WAIT!" Margo pointed across the deck. "What's that?"

A pink bubble was growing on the surface of the trash pile. Shivers and Margo slogged over to it as fast as they could. The bubble was getting bigger.

"AAGH! The trash is growing!" Shivers screamed.

Margo reached out and carefully touched the bubble. Then she realized she couldn't untouch it. It was very sticky. "Bubble gum!" she exclaimed. She tried to pull her hand away, but the bubble came with it. As she lifted it from the surface, she saw that there was something dangling from it. And that something was a blowfish.

"Albee!" Shivers cheered. "I didn't know you liked bubble gum!" He gave Albee a big hug. As he squeezed Albee, the bubble got bigger. Then Margo squeezed the bubble and Albee got bigger, puffing up to his full blowfish size. Surprised, Shivers squeezed Albee again and the bubble got bigger. Then Margo squeezed the bubble again, and—well, you get the idea. This went on for so long that Shelly had to interrupt.

"Shouldn't that fish be in water?" Shelly asked. During his adventure, Albee had lost his bag.

Shelly filled an old soda bottle with water and tossed it to Margo. She popped Albee inside and screwed on the cap.

Albee sighed. "I just hate losing my bag when I travel." Then he swam in a circle around the bottle. "But this will do."

Of course, no one heard him.

"Come on, Shivers, we've got to get back to the *Groundhog*," said Margo.

"You're right," said Shivers. "The ghost of Quincy Thomas is coming after me, and there's nothing here for us but moldy fruit and heartache."

"And toenails," said Shelly. "Don't forget the toenails."

"What?!" Shivers's eyes blew up bigger than Albee's bubble.

Shelly shrugged. "This ship is, like, half toenails."

Shivers barged across the barge, splashing through the trash as fast as his own little toes would take him, then jumped off the edge of the ship. He was so terrified of the toenails that he forgot to be afraid of the ocean below. As the choppy water sloshed over his head, he remembered.

Margo leaped in after him, clutching Albee tightly. "Good-bye, Smelly!" she called as she plummeted through the air.

"It's Shelly!"

Margo grabbed onto Shivers's hand and tried to swim toward the *Groundhog*. But just then, they heard a creaking sound from below the surface. A giant metal cage rose from the sea and scooped them up. The lid snapped shut above their heads. They were trapped inside.

CHAPTER SEVEN

SHIVERS GRIPPED THE METAL bars of the trap and shook them as hard as he could, but they wouldn't budge. "AAAAAGH! We're locked in!" he screamed.

The trap lifted up into the air, bouncing Shivers, Margo, and Albee around like beach balls in a blender. It jolted higher and higher, smashing and spinning them in circles. Red blurs whizzed by, but they were so dizzy it was impossible to tell what they were. Finally the trap stopped climbing and their somersaults came to a halt. As the swirling slowed, Shivers's eyes regained focus and he saw what had been bouncing around inside with them.

"Lobsters!" he shrieked. The trap was full of them, clicking their claws and climbing all over the place.

Suddenly, the trap tipped over and the top sprang open. Shivers, Margo, Albee, and the lobsters fell out faster than a fly who can't flap. They landed with a THWAP! on a perfectly polished wooden floor. Margo and Shivers leaped away from the lobsters as quickly as they could, looking around frantically.

They were on the deck of the most magnificent ship either of them had ever seen.

The hull was as white as a freshly brushed tooth. The railings were dazzling gold. Even the lobster trap seemed to be shimmering sterling silver.

Soon they heard footsteps behind them and two men appeared wearing starched white shirts with matching gloves, jet-black suit jackets dotted with shiny silver buttons, and small golden pocket watches. They were each carrying a copper lobster bucket. When they saw Shivers and Margo, they dropped the buckets to the floor with a CLANG! and crossed their arms angrily.

"Children in the lobster haul?!" said one of the men.

"Again?!" the other guffawed. "Well, they must belong to one of the passengers. I'll have them carted off immediately." He clapped his hands briskly and shouted, "TOBIAS!"

Instantly, a man drove up on a golf cart. He was dressed exactly the same as the other two men, except he had a gleaming gold badge on his jacket that said CAPTAIN.

Tobias quickly but carefully whisked Margo and Shivers into the back of his cart. Then he picked up Albee's bottle and placed him delicately in the cup holder. He stepped on the gas and the cart zoomed off.

Shivers marveled at Tobias's gold badge. "Are you the captain of this ship?" he asked.

"I'm the captain of the butlers," Tobias explained in an English accent that made him sound very fancy. "It's much more important."

Shivers and Margo turned to each other, looking puzzled. They had never seen a ship with a butler, let alone so many butlers that they needed a captain.

"How many butlers *are* there?" asked Margo.

"Two for every passenger, of course," Tobias replied without hesitation. "This is the biggest, most expensive yacht on the sea."

"What's a yacht?" Shivers whispered to Margo.

She thought for a second. "It's a fancy boat that fancy people ride on to get away from it all."

"Get away from what?! Is something chasing them?!" Shivers was alarmed.

"No! I mean, they come out here to relax."

"They go out to sea to *relax*? That's crazy!" Shivers squealed. "I can think of a *lot* of places more relaxing than this giant bowl of fish poop."

Before Shivers could start listing those places, Tobias drove the golf cart through a swinging door and screeched to a halt inside a majestic ballroom full of people who *did* look very relaxed. In

fact, they weren't moving or speaking at all. They were sitting drowsily in overstuffed armchairs topped with frilly pillows. Crystal chandeliers dangled from the ceiling above them. The walls were peppered with paintings of brightly colored shapes smashing into each other. A plaque above the paintings read THIS IS ART.

There was so much to look at that all Shivers could do was gasp.

Tobias whipped around and held up his

hand. "Please don't gasp! The air in here is very expensive."

Tobias grabbed Shivers and Margo by their wrists and led them to a corner of the room sectioned off by a red velvet rope. He unhooked the rope and ushered Shivers and Margo behind it, then clicked it back into place.

"You stay here in the Lost and Found," he instructed, taking off his white gloves and tossing them in a trash can. In a flash, he pulled a new pair from his pocket and put them on.

"You can't leave us in the Lost and Found!" said Margo.

"Do you know where you are?" Tobias asked.

"No," she admitted.

"So you're lost and I found you. Sounds like the perfect fit. I'm sure your parents will come get you after the party is over. Toodle-loo!" Tobias waved and hopped back into the golf cart. "Don't forget your fish!" he said, tossing Albee's bottle to Margo. Then he sped away.

Shivers slumped his shoulders and said, "Oh, great! This day gets better and better! There's a ghost trying to kill me. We still haven't found any treasure. And now we have to wait for our *parents* to pick us up?!"

"Snap out of it!" she said, shaking the rope. "What we really need to do right now is find some treasure."

"How are we supposed to find treasure? I can't even think straight with all this jewelry clinking and clanging. And those priceless paintings on the wall are so distracting. What do they even mean? And don't get me started on that giant diamond sitting by itself on the windowsill. There's so much glare on that thing I can barely see!"

"SHIVERS!" Margo interrupted him. "Do you hear what you're saying? There's treasure everywhere!" She was grinning like a raccoon at a trash buffet. "We just have to figure out how to get it." She pointed to a pointy-nosed woman with big red earrings. "We could try to swipe those ruby earrings."

Shivers hopped up and down, clapping his hands. "We could pickpocket the pocket watch from that prickly old man."

"If we're quick enough maybe we could snatch the solid-gold vase from on top of that piano over there." She gestured to a gigantic grand piano on the other side of the ballroom.

Shivers clutched her arm. "Margo, you're a genius!"

Margo blushed. "The vase isn't *that* good of an idea."

"SONG AND DANCE TIME!" Shivers shouted. "That'll cheer me up!"

Albee smacked his fin to his fishy little forehead.

Margo stuttered, "What? No! I didn't mean–"

But Shivers was already halfway across the room, marching toward the piano like a soldier. Or like someone in a marching band. Right now, Shivers felt like a little bit of both. *If this is going to be my last day on earth and I'm going to spend the rest of time in the gut of a ghost, I'm not going down without some singing and dancing,* he thought.

Margo and Albee looked on in horror as Shivers pulled out the piano bench, sat down, and plinked out a high note.

Immediately, the woman with the ruby earrings looked up in shock and ruffled the feathers of her ostrich coat. "You there! Get your grubby child hands away from that priceless piano!"

"Agreed!" said a man with silver hair, jabbing a jewel-encrusted cane at Shivers.

"AGH! A walking stick!" Shivers screamed.

"It's not a walking stick, it's a sitting stick! Don't make me make my butler get my walking stick!" The man scowled.

Shivers reached out and touched the keys longingly. "But no one's even played this piano! It's covered in dust!"

"No one knows how to play that old thing," said the silver-haired man. "We just keep it here so no one else can play it."

"But an unplayed piano is like an unpopped

kernel of popcorn. You never know what magic you're missing!" Shivers argued.

Shivers quickly shook out his hands, then held them up to his face to give them a little pep talk. "All right, fingers. You fing, and I'll sing."

Then he raised his hands in the air and crashed them down on the keys, striking a chord that jolted the passengers out of their glazed stupor.

"What did I say about touching that piano?" the woman in the ruby earrings barked.

But then Shivers launched into a rhythm so captivating that the passengers couldn't help but start to groove in their armchairs, squirming around like restless babies in car seats. Their mouth muscles curled up into creaky grins.

"That's the best ivory-tickling I've seen since I paid to play with an elephant on safari last summer!" a man said as two butlers lifted him to his feet. "Dance me!" he commanded, and the butlers twisted his hips for him.

One by one, the passengers demanded help

getting up from their chairs. As they started to sway, Margo heard the jingling and jangling of gold-plated bracelets and sapphire-encrusted shoelaces. She had a feeling this song and dance time might pay off soon.

Shivers was really hitting his stride. He pounded out a beat with his left hand and worked melody magic with his right. Then he took a deep breath and let out the most beautiful note his screamy mouth knew how to sing.

"He sings better than my chorus of canaries," one of the passengers exclaimed, throwing her hands in the air with delight. As she wiggled her wrists up and down to the rhythm, Margo saw an enormous emerald ring slide down her finger and nearly fall to the floor. Suddenly, she knew exactly what she had to do.

She ran over to Shivers and whispered, "They're loving your singing but you've got to get them dancing! After all, this is song and *dance* time." She placed Albee on the piano for extra encouragement.

"You're right!" Shivers said, his eyes lighting up. "Without the dancing, the singing is just a lonely cry for attention." Then he stood up from the piano bench, all the while continuing to play, and called out to the crowd, "Everybody repeat after me!"

"Everybody repeat after me!" the crowd called back.

"No, not yet!" yelled Shivers.

"No, not yet!" shouted the crowd.

Shivers realized this might have been a bad idea. He decided to rephrase. "Do as I do!"

The silver-haired man looked confused. "You want us to become a small, filthy boy with a funny hat?"

Shivers let out an exasperated sigh.

Margo cupped her hands in front of her mouth and shouted, "Just dance like him!"

Shivers tickled out a new melody on the keys and tapped his right foot to the beat. The passengers tapped their feet to the beat, too, but they ended up looking like they were waiting impatiently for something. Shivers decided to speed up the song, and he tapped out a jig with both of his feet. The crowd tried to keep up, even though some of them were still trying to *stand* up. All the jigging was making the jewelry jangle even louder and Margo knew that something had to slip loose soon. She saw a stout woman in a shimmering party dress flapping her feet so fast it looked like she was hopping on hot coals. She clapped her hands in the air so carelessly that she didn't even notice when her clapping turned to unclasping. Her solid-gold watch flew off her wrist and into the air. Margo ran to catch it, holding out her hands, but the stout woman took that as an invitation to dance. She grabbed Margo's hands and they danced a polka across the room.

Shivers was having the time of his life. This was quite possibly the most successful song and dance time he had ever hosted. But that's because it was usually just him and Albee, and Albee was a terrible dancer.

It was time to kick it up a notch—with lots of kicking! Shivers flung his feet high in the air while spinning his arms around like windmills, all without missing a note on the piano.

The passengers kicked as high as their plump little legs could go, flailing their arms like baby birds failing to fly. The whole ballroom was bustling with swinging hips and stomping feet. The silver-haired man shouted, "Get me my dancing stick!"

Margo had finally gotten rid of the polka woman, and she darted through the line of kicking legs toward a lady whose pearl necklace was bouncing around wildly on her neck. Margo quietly climbed onto an armchair behind her and tried to pluck the necklace off her, like a ring toss in reverse. But before she could grab it, the woman whirled around and gasped. "Look, everyone, this small child wants a piggyback ride"—she smiled wistfully—"just like my daughter used to before I forgot where I put her!" The woman heaved Margo onto her back, then continued her high kicking.

Even the butlers were beginning to dance. One of them noticed that Shivers didn't have a dance partner, so he wiggled his way over to the piano. But as soon as he got there, he scrunched up his nose and started coughing.

"What is that ghastly smell?" the butler blurted, backing away briskly.

Shivers was confused. Then he took a big sniff of the air around him and a horrible smell crept its way right into his nose.

I was so busy singing, I didn't notice I was in a stink cloud! he thought.

He wondered what the smell was and where it was coming from. He tried to snort out the

source, but he couldn't find it and he didn't know how much more of the thick, moldy odor he could handle.

His piano playing began to fall apart. He smashed his fingers sloppily on the keys.

"Play faster, Shivers!" Margo urged. "Keep 'em dancing!"

Shivers played faster and faster. The smell was making him frantic. He pinched his nose and shook his head—anything to make the stink extinct. But he couldn't escape it. The passengers were mimicking his every move and the dance floor was deteriorating into chaos. Margo rolled off the woman's shoulders. She squeezed through the bumping bodies and bouncing bellies. All of a sudden, she saw the silver-haired man thrust his hip into the piano. The solid-gold vase slid across the shiny black surface, then wobbled dangerously on the edge. Just as the wobble turned into a topple, Margo dove across the dance floor. She reached out her hands and caught the vase right before it clanged against the ground.

Margo quickly unzipped her big green backpack and stuffed the vase inside, sandwiching it between the pirate book and . . . a sandwich. She was about to zip it back up when the music came to a screeching stop—and Shivers's screeching came to a sudden start.

"IT'S THE GHOST!" he screamed, leaping

up from the piano bench. "IT'S THE STINKY, SMELLY GHOST!"

The passengers were frozen in stunned silence as Shivers ran over to Margo and wailed, "Quincy Thomas is getting closer! It's just like the curse said. I'm smelling his foul odor everywhere I go!" In his panic, Shivers grabbed Margo by the arms. He shook her shoulders and the gold vase came tumbling out of her backpack. It hit the floor with a loud GONG! that echoed off the ballroom's marble walls.

The woman with the ruby earrings pointed her finger sharply. "These aren't children. They're tiny thieves!"

The crowd gasped.

The silver-haired man put down his dancing stick and picked up his shouting stick. He jabbed it in the air and commanded, "RELEASE THE HOUNDS!"

CHAPTER EIGHT

SHIVERS FELT A LOW rumble beneath his feet. He could hear the stampede of angry dogs tearing down the deck toward the ballroom. He could imagine the saliva spilling from their jagged teeth as they readied themselves for an afternoon snack of petrified pirate.

"Prepare to meet our attack dogs!" the silver-haired man cackled.

All Shivers could think to do was close his eyes, cover his face with his hands, and hope that Margo tasted better than he did.

SLAM!

The pack of dogs careened through the

swinging door and spilled into the ballroom. Shivers couldn't bear to look, but in an instant, he heard the most unexpected noise—laughter. And it was coming from Margo.

Shivers peeked between two fingers to see what was so funny.

"Poodles!" Margo guffawed. "They're poodles!"

And they really were! Fluffy white poodles no bigger than bunnies, with puffs of fur on the tops of their heads and the tips of their tails so it looked like they'd just come out of a cotton candy machine. They were all wearing different doggie outfits, each more ridiculous than the last. One wore a tuxedo and top hat. Another wore a bedazzled T-shirt that said *Top Dog*. There was

even one poodle in a full tennis outfit, including tennis shoes and a miniature racket.

Shivers couldn't help but smile at the sight of the poodle parade. "Hey, little buddy!" he said, reaching out to pet one of the dogs.

But just then, Tobias, the captain of the butlers, appeared in the doorway. "ATTACK!" he commanded, pointing at Shivers and Margo.

In an instant, the poodles stopped looking like baby bunnies and started looking like rabid rabbits. They bared their teeth and snapped their jaws.

Margo snatched up the golden vase and Shivers snatched up Albee. "RUN!" they both shouted at the same time.

They scrambled between the passengers and bounced off different butlers, making their way toward a door at the back of the ballroom. The dogs scurried behind them, yipping and nipping at their heels.

"This way!" Margo said, flinging open the door. Shivers followed and tried to close the door behind him, but there were too many poodles pushing their way through.

They ran down a long hallway with elegant green carpeting. The poodles squeezed their way through the hall behind them, pouncing over each other like they were playing leap dog.

"Margo, get me out of here! This hall room is even scarier than the ballroom!" Shivers shrieked.

"In here!" Margo said, running through the first door she could find. The door led to the ship's spa, where all the passengers went to relax and unwind after a long day of laxing and winding. The room was dimly lit and dotted with flickering candles that smelled like peaches. It was completely quiet except for the soothing sound of whale calls piping in through speakers. Passengers lay around in one big sudsy hot tub with slices of cucumber sitting on their eyes. Butlers fed them huge slices of cake whenever they opened their mouths.

"Margo, where are we? This is the most

terrifying place I've ever seen!" Shivers said skittishly. "Haven't these people heard of night-lights? Why is it so dimly lit?"

"Because we're *trying* to relax!" said a lady in the tub with a towel wrapped tightly around her tiny head.

Shivers's jaw dropped open at the sight of her, as he mistook the cucumbers on her face for giant green eyeballs. "ALIEN!" he shrieked. "THEY'RE ALL ALIENS!"

"Sir, you'll have to calm down," said one of the butlers. "Here, have a slice of cake."

"What?! Cake?!? Again?!? Don't you know I get *C*-sick!" Shivers batted the piece of cake out of the butler's hand.

"We've got to go!" Margo urged, grabbing Shivers's sleeve. She could hear the poodles' yips getting closer.

"Wait!" Shivers cupped his hand over his ear. "Is that the sound of whales? THERE ARE WHALES IN THE TUB!"

"Whales?!" the passengers screamed as they flailed in the tub, sloshing soapy water everywhere.

"Oh no! Spilled suds!" the butlers cried, grabbing huge buckets.

By now, all the wailing about whales had attracted the poodles' attention and they came bounding into the spa.

Margo and Shivers tried to make a run for it, but they slipped and slid all over the floor, which was soaked in soapy bathwater.

Albee slid around in his bottle, too, but that was pretty normal.

Just as a poodle was about to make a chew toy out of Shivers's bunny slippers, a butler scooped the dog into his bucket, thinking it was a ball of bubbles. In fact, because the poodles were so fluffy, none of the butlers were able to tell the difference between them and the foamy bubbles on the floor. They flung the suds—and the poodles—back into the tub.

"GO!" Margo shouted, pushing Shivers forward. They skidded out a side door, leaving behind a spa full of soaking poodles, splashing passengers, and befuddled butlers babbling about bubbles. There was cucumber and cake everywhere.

As the door swung closed behind Shivers and Margo, they looked around and saw that they were now in the ship's hair salon. The place was packed with passengers in the middle of manicures and makeovers.

Shivers was amazed. He took off his feathered pirate cap, revealing a matted mess. "Margo, look! They could turn my hair *don't* into a hair *do*!"

He jumped up into an empty leather chair.

"I want something new but not *scary* new," he told the stylist.

"You got it, kid," she said, filling her hands with sticky hair gel and squashing it onto Shivers's scalp.

Just then, the pack of freshly bathed poodles pounced through the door. They may have been cleaner than before, but the bubble bath had certainly done nothing to relax them. They marched through the piles of hair on the floor, baring their teeth and staring furiously at Shivers, Margo, and Albee.

Margo knew she didn't have a second to spare. She held the golden vase in one hand and grabbed a hair dryer with the other. She pointed the dryer down, then turned it on full force. The blast of warm wind hit the ground, swirling a storm of hair up into the poodles' faces. They stopped in their tracks, blinded by the hair-icane.

"This way, Shivers!" Margo shouted over the whir of the dryer. She backed up across the room, still holding the dryer out in front of her, until she felt a metal doorknob behind her. In one quick motion, she opened the door, ran through it, and found herself standing in the sunlight on the main deck.

Without skipping a beat, she held the stolen golden vase up in the air triumphantly.

"We did it, Shivers! Now let's get back to the *Groundhog*." She started to run down the deck, but stopped when she heard the sound of . . . nothing. She spun around to see that she was all alone. "Shivers?"

She started to worry. What had happened to Shivers and Albee at the hands—or paws—of those poodles?

Suddenly, there was a screech of tiny wheels as Tobias skidded around the corner in his golf cart.

"Ho, ho! Found you! As I always say, when someone steals a vase, Tobias will crack the case!" he said proudly.

He marched over to Margo, his perfectly polished shoes clacking loudly on the wooden deck. He sneered as he stood over her and snatched the vase from her hand. He took one look at it and scoffed. "Well, this will have to go straight into the furnace."

Margo was confused. "The furnace? Why?"

"Now that your grubby little kid claws have touched it, I'll have to melt it down and reshape it into a new vase." Tobias tossed the vase into a chute marked FURNACE.

Margo watched in horror as her only hope of saving Shivers disappeared like a poodle in a bubble bath.

Tobias grabbed Margo by her wrist. "Now, what to do with you? And what happened to your filthy little friend?"

Just then, they heard a squeal of delight followed by a scream of fright as Shivers burst through the door looking a lot more like a poodle than

a pirate. His hair was sculpted into a big fuzzy puff ball on the top of his head.

The poodles chased after him, each with their own new hairstyle. As Shivers tried to out-run the dogs, he yipped and yelped, bounding around the deck, and generally looked like a poorly trained puppy.

"You!" Tobias shouted, pointing right at Shivers. "Stay right there!"

If Shivers had a tail, it would have been between his legs. He was so frightened he couldn't even speak; he could only whimper.

The poodles felt so bad for him that they all crowded around in whim-pathy. With his new hairdo, Shivers blended in perfectly with the pack.

Tobias marched over and sneered down at Shivers. "Stupid poodle! Why aren't you wearing a collar?" He pulled a jewel-encrusted collar out of his jacket pocket and snapped it around Shivers's neck.

Then he turned back to Margo. "Now, as I was saying, where is your filthy friend?"

"Shivers, let's go!" Margo said. She was sitting in the driver's seat of the golf cart. She honked the tiny horn and Shivers leaped to his feet.

"It's you!" Tobias gasped.

But Shivers was already in the passenger seat.

As the golf cart zipped away, Tobias shook his fist. "Melt down the collar! Melt down the golf cart! Melt down the whole ship!" he shouted, melting down himself.

Margo whipped the cart around a corner.

"When did you learn how to drive a golf cart?" Shivers asked.

"About ten seconds after I stole it," said Margo.

They came to a screeching stop in front of the lobster trap.

Margo scrambled into the big metal cage. "Quick! Get in!"

Shivers and Albee squeezed in next to her.

She reached through the bars and pulled on the cables holding the trap, lowering them down as fast as she could.

Shivers noticed that Margo's hands were suspiciously empty. "What happened to the vase?" he asked.

"Tobias took it," Margo muttered, panting as she yanked at the cables.

"He did?! What are we going to bury at the ghost grave?!" The stink of failure hung in the air—or maybe it was just the stink of Quincy Thomas, reminding Shivers that he was getting closer by the minute.

"You don't really think I would have let us leave that yacht empty-handed, do you?" Margo said with a smirk. "You're wearing the biggest piece of treasure I've ever seen right now."

"My bunny slippers? They *are* one of a kind." He looked down at his feet. "Well, two of a kind."

"No!" Margo laughed. "That collar!"

Shivers took off the collar and saw that it was covered in brightly colored jewels surrounding an enormous diamond. His eyes grew so wide he almost cried. "Margo, you are the greatest friend I could ever hope for."

Margo wanted to soak up the moment, but she realized they were about to get soaked themselves. "Hold on! We're about to hit the water!"

"AAAGH! Water!" Shivers screamed, looping the collar around his wrist and holding onto Albee with one hand and onto the bars with the other.

"Sorry, Shivers, this is going to ruin your new haircut," said Margo.

"Oh, no! I don't want to say toodle-loo to my poodle 'do!"

SPLASH!

Margo and Shivers came up sopping wet, their hair stringy and stuck to their faces. Albee looked pretty much the same.

CHAPTER NINE

MARGO AND ALBEE WERE the first ones to make it back to the *Groundhog* after a very long journey. They were both expert swimmers, and were able to cut through the foamy waves like a hot knife through butter. Shivers wasn't a very strong swimmer, but he was an expert panicker. He flailed and thrashed his way through the current until he eventually made it to the ship.

He pulled himself up onto the deck and collapsed, huffing with exhaustion.

"Somebody please tell me it's nap time," Shivers groaned.

"Nope! It's map time!" Margo said, standing

over him excitedly. "We can finally chart our course for the Cape of Cods now that we have our treasure!"

Shivers took the treasure out of his coat pocket and looked at it with amazement. "Wow! This is the biggest diamond I've ever seen! It shimmers with the light of a thousand song and dance times!"

He turned the collar around in his hands. "So this is a dog collar. Having a pet must be really expensive."

"Don't you already have a pet?" Margo asked, holding up Albee.

Shivers narrowed his eyes. "Albee's not my pet, he's my first mate! Could a pet do what he's doing right now?"

"What's he doing?"
Margo asked.

"Supervising!" Albee
and Shivers shouted
at the same time.

"Right. Sorry." She patted Albee's bottle, then turned to Shivers. "Now put that collar away. We've got to get moving!" She hopped up to the helm and pulled *The Pirate Book You've Been Looking For* out of her big green backpack. She flipped to the page with the map and steered the ship on a hard course for the Cape of Cods.

The sun was beginning to set, turning the clouds in the sky a fiery orange. Shivers ran up to the captain's deck next to Margo. "How long until we get there?" he asked nervously. "My birthday is almost here!"

"Don't worry, we'll make it in time," Margo assured him.

A sharp wind swirled around Shivers, sending a stinky breeze into his nostrils. "This ghost must be getting close; his awful stench is getting worse!"

Margo scrunched up her nose. "It *is* pretty bad." She turned to the page with Quincy Thomas's curse. "Remember, the foul odor is just the first sign of the curse. After that, you're supposed to become as merciless and violent as he was."

"Does that mean I'll have to use a sword?" Shivers cringed. "They're so *pointy*."

Margo laughed. "I don't think you have to worry about it just yet."

As the *Groundhog* pushed its way farther north, the water became more and more choppy. The waves were so wobbly that Margo had to grip the helm tightly just to steer. Shivers lay on the deck, trying his best not to puke. He needed something to distract him from the angry waves, the darkening sky, and the general sense of doom hanging over his head like a sad sombrero. He picked up the pirate book and leafed through the section on Pirate Zeroes. Each page described a different pirate who had, in one way or another, failed spectacularly at sailing the Seven Seas.

"Look at this guy!" Shivers said, pointing to a picture of a pirate with a big belly and an even bigger beard. "Snack Beard!" he read aloud. "A pirate so consumed by snacking that he had no time for plundering. His beard became so full of crumbs that one day, he was carried away by hungry seagulls, and he was never seen again."

Shivers shook his head. "Talk about a snack attack." He flipped to the next page. "Awww!" he squealed, looking at a picture of the cutest pirate he had ever seen. He was small and pudgy with big bright cheeks and a button nose. "Cutie Pie!" Shivers read, showing the picture to Margo. "With the face of an angel and the temper of a two-year-old, Cutie Pie was too stinkin' cute to be a pirate. After being laughed at one too many times, he threw an enormous and adorable fit. He stomped off angrily and was never seen again."

Shivers shook his head in disbelief. "I can't believe there are so many pirate losers in here." He turned the page and read on. "Shivers the Pirate." His jaw nearly dropped to the ground. "WHAT?!"

Margo whipped her head around. "What did you say?"

"It's me!" Shivers said with dismay, staring at a picture of himself cowering in a corner. He read on, his voice quivering, "Shivers the Pirate is the scarediest pirate to never sail the Seven Seas. Perhaps the biggest pirate zero of all time, he has been totally terrified of everything since the moment he was born. He lives a wimpy, screamy life on his ship that never leaves the sand." Shivers closed the book sadly. "Biggest pirate zero of all time?" he murmured.

Margo ripped the book from his hands and chucked it down to the dance deck, where it landed with a clatter. "That's not true!" she shouted, fuming like a fire ant. "You've set sail, you've battled snails, you've even saved my life! You're not a zero; you're a hero!"

"No, I'm not. The whole world thinks I'm just a giant scaredy-cat." Shivers shuddered. The image of a giant cat gave him the creeps.

"It doesn't matter. Only *you* can make yourself a hero," Margo said firmly. "I heard that at a sandwich shop after all the cooks quit."

Shivers wasn't convinced. "How could anyone as scared as me be a hero?" he asked, looking around. "I'm afraid of every wave that rocks the boat. I'm afraid of the sun setting and forgetting to come back up. I'm afraid of those two strange pirates standing on the deck. . . ."

Margo's eyes popped open wide. For once, she screamed as loud as Shivers did.

"AGGGGHHH!"

They both bolted to the railing of the captain's deck and looked down.

"Who are you?!" Margo demanded.

"We're the Ransom brothers!" shouted the men.

"I'm Handsome Ransom," said the one on the right. He was tall and lean with thick sculpted hair that sat on top of his perfectly shaped skull. He wore a light blue pirate blouse with billowing sleeves, tight tan trousers, and polished black boots. His smile was as bright and dazzling as a camera flash.

Then the one on the left piped up, "And I'm Footsome Ransom!" Footsome was as hideous as his brother was gorgeous. His head looked like an old olive, saggy and tinged with green. His clothes were crumpled and crusted with crud. He tried to smile, but greasy spit leaked through his charred brown teeth and down his chin.

"We're twin brothers!" Footsome said. He pushed a loose piece of earwax back into his ear. "But I'm sure you already guessed that."

Before Margo could say anything, Handsome asked, "Who are you?"

"I'm Margo. And this is Shivers the Pirate. We demand to know what you're doing on our ship!"

"We're here to take your treasure, of course!" said Handsome. "That's what pirates do!" He beamed.

Thinking quickly, Margo lied. "We don't have any treasure!"

"A likely story! Every pirate ship has treasure. We'll just have to find it," growled Footsome. He pointed to the top of the mast. "Perhaps it's hidden in the crow's nest!"

"Good thinking, brother!" said Handsome. "You climb up and check, while I take a look at this dashing fellow I keep seeing in the waves."

As Footsome climbed up to the crow's nest and Handsome leaned over the railing to stare at his own reflection in the water, Shivers and Margo looked at each other in a panic. They had to hide their one piece of treasure, and they had to do it fast.

Shivers stumbled down the captain's deck stairs and ran inside the ship. He gripped the dog collar tightly as he looked around for a hiding place. He decided to stash it in the first place he could think of: the pantry. He gently stuffed it between two pieces of pita bread, then quietly closed the door.

By the time Shivers got back to the deck, Footsome was shouting from the crow's nest, "No treasure up here! It's just full of dirt!"

"Of course it is!" Shivers shouted back. "I use

that thing as a giant daisy pot!"

Footsome groaned and pulled himself out of the soil. "Did you find anything down there, brother?" he called.

"Yes, I found a new way to smile and wink at the same time!" said Handsome as he gazed longingly at his own reflection.

Margo swung down from the captain's deck and planted herself firmly in front of Handsome. "I told you, we don't have any treasure here!" she insisted.

"Nobody lies to the Ransom brothers!" Footsome sneered as he scrambled down from the crow's nest. "Come on, let's turn this place upside down!"

The brothers barged past Shivers and Margo and headed inside the ship.

Shivers followed close—but not too close—behind, crying out, "No! Everything has to stay right-side up!" Then he thought for a second. "Except for my hourglass! That thing could use a good turn!"

Handsome and Footsome stomped into

Shivers's sleeping quarters. They spotted a magnificent wooden chest at the foot of his bed.

"Jackpot!" said Handsome, kicking open the chest. He reached inside greedily, but when he pulled out his fist, it was just full of–"Popcorn?!" he balked. "Why do you keep your popcorn in a treasure chest?!"

Shivers looked at him like he was crazy. "Because it's the treasure of the food world!" Then Footsome saw a big piggy bank sitting on a shelf. "Aha!" He grabbed it and smashed it to the ground.

But instead of coins, a pile of tiny plastic piggies spilled out. Now it was Footsome who looked at Shivers like he was crazy.

"Well, what do *you* keep in a piggy bank?" Shivers said.

Exasperated, the two men tore down the hallway. Footsome stuck his head in the shower and thought he found gold—but it was really just mold. He often confused the two.

Handsome sifted through the mop closet but all he found was—well, you know.

There was only one room left unsearched: the kitchen. Handsome and Footsome charged in, fuming with frustration. They turned over the table and toppled the chairs. All Shivers could do was look on in terror and hope that they didn't think to check in the pantry. But that hope was dashed immediately. As Handsome reached for the pantry doorknob, Shivers knew he had to act fast. Just outside the kitchen, the pirate book was lying open on the deck.

Without thinking, Shivers darted outside, picked up the book, and threw it as hard as he could. It sailed through the air and a single page sliced the tip of Handsome's nose.

"MY FACE! MY BEAUTIFUL FACE!" Handsome wailed. On the very edge of his nose was a teeny tiny papercut. He fell to the floor and pointed up at Shivers, shouting, "WHAT HAVE YOU DONE TO ME?!"

Footsome lifted Handsome to his feet. "We need to get you to a doctor. We'll have to find treasure some other time!"

As Handsome hobbled out onto the deck, he sobbed, "But Quincy Thomas is going to kill us...."

"Quincy Thomas?! You're cursed, too?" Shivers asked.

"Of course! Look around you! Everyone in this cape is cursed! You think all these other ships are just sailing here for a Cod Party?!" Footsome spat.

Shivers and Margo looked around, and for

the first time they noticed that the sea was crowded with pirate ships, all sailing at full speed toward the craggly cape jutting out in the dark distance ahead.

Handsome yelled to Shivers, "If the ghost of Quincy Thomas kills me, my ghost will come and haunt you! And you'll know it's me because I'll be an *extremely* good-looking ghost!"

"You'll pay for this, Shivers the Pirate!" Footsome said, pointing a crooked finger at him.

Then the Ransom brothers swung over the railing and disappeared into the night.

Shivers gulped. "Well, that was my least favorite part of the day."

He ran into the kitchen and opened the pantry. The collar was still tucked inside its bread bed. "I'm just glad they didn't ask for a pita, butter, and jelly sandwich," he said.

"Nice going, Shivers!" Margo cheered, patting him on the back. "You sliced him up good!"

All the color drained from his face until he was as pale as a dove's tail. "Margo! It's happening! I've become as violent and merciless as Quincy Thomas!" He fell to the deck and screamed, "I'm going to be ghost toast!!"

CHAPTER TEN

MARGO STEERED THE SHIP into the Cape of Cods, trying not to collide with the fleet of other pirate ships all making their frightened way toward the coastline. The sky had turned from a menacing red to a haunting purple to a totally terrifying, soul-sucking black.

Shivers flopped around the dance deck like a frantic fish.

"Shivers, stop freaking out! We're almost at the Cape!" Margo said.

"But we're running out of time! Quincy Thomas is closer than ever! Look at the signs! One: I smell him everywhere I go. Two: I've become violent and merciless. And three . . . what's number three again?"

"There is no number three. You'll be dead by then," Margo called down to him.

"AAAAAAAAAAAAAAAAAAGH!!!!!!!!!!!!"

And with the piercing sound of Shivers's screeching, Margo decided it was time to finally drop the anchor. She joined Shivers on the dance deck and pulled him up to his feet. "We're here," she said.

They looked out over the railing and saw a stretch of sandy beach in front of them. A crescent moon was cresting in the sky, casting an eerie white light across the jagged rocks that lined the cape. Dozens of ships bobbed

nearby, while pirate crews hauled crates of treasure onto the shore.

Soon they heard the flutter of flapping wings above them, and a flock of parrots flew toward them.

Shivers covered his head and cried, "AAAAGH! Flying copycats!"

Shivers hated parrots. They had no sense of humor. He once tried to tell a parrot a knock-knock joke but he could never get to the punchline. It was just knock-knocking for days. The parrots landed on the railing and Shivers realized that these were the most terrifying birds he'd ever seen. Their feathers were white, their talons were white, their beaks were white, and even their thick ugly tongues were white.

Shivers gulped in horror. "Ghost parrots!"

One by one, the parrots began to speak.

"Wait until dark," squawked the first one.

Shivers cocked his head, confused.

Then the second bird screeched, "Go to the haunted graveyard."

"They're giving us instructions!" whispered Margo.

"Bury your treasure at the grave of Quincy Thomas the Pirate," the third one said, fluffing its feathers.

The last one chimed in, "Run away screaming and never return."

Then the whole flock spoke in an ear-scraping chorus. "Once your treasure has been processed, you will be one-hundred-percent uncursed."

With that, they lifted back up into the air and flew to the next ship.

Shivers turned to Margo and slapped her on the back. "Well, Margo, you heard the parrots. Have fun! And don't take too long, my birthday is a few hours away." He curled up on the dance deck. "If you need to find me, follow the sweet sounds of sleep. Good night!"

Margo scowled. "In your dreams, buddy!"

"That's exactly my point," he said, closing his eyes.

"Shivers, you can't fake this. No one can uncurse you but you," she said sternly. She picked up Albee's bottle, swung on her big green backpack, and headed for the shore.

Shivers groaned and sat up. He patted his coat pocket to make sure the dog collar was still there. Then he ran up next to Margo. They waded through the shallow water until they reached the beach. There was a tall wooden sign in the sand that said HAUNTED GRAVEYARD THIS WAY, with an arrow pointing toward a thicket of overgrown trees.

Shivers put one bunny slipper in front of the other as he marched quickly through the sand. Margo was right behind him.

Shivers looked back at her. "Do I have to lead the whole way?"

As he said that, he didn't see the giant hole in his way. He took a step forward and felt nothing but nothingness beneath his bunny slippers.

He screeched as he plummeted downward. Margo reached out just in time to grab his hand as he dangled over the deep darkness.

"HELP!" Shivers shouted, trying to get a foothold. "Who knew bunny slippers would be so slippery?!"

Margo dug her heels into the sand. She pulled so hard she thought her arms might pop off. Finally Shivers came flying out of the abyss and they both landed in a heap.

"What *was* that?" Shivers asked, shaking the sand out of his hair.

Margo found a small sign next to the gaping hole. THE BOTTOMLESS PIT OF DESPAIR: WHERE QUINCY THOMAS THROWS THE BONES OF HIS VICTIMS.

"AAGGH! A bone bucket!" Shivers quivered.

They sidestepped the hole and made their way to the edge of the forest. A narrow path cut through the trees. Margo knelt down to read a plaque on the ground.

THE PATH OF LOST SOULS:
WHERE DOOMED PIRATES
TAKE THEIR LAST STEPS

Shivers let out a loud, shrill squeak like a mouse with a microphone, but they had to move forward.

Shivers gripped Margo's arm. As they made their way down the path, they suddenly found themselves in a sticky situation. With each step

Shivers took, it became harder and harder to peel his bunny slippers off the path.

"I can't move!" Shivers cried. "Quincy Thomas is gluing me to the ground!"

"Me, too!" said Margo. Her shoes were just as stuck.

"Albee, go on without us," Shivers moaned.

"Wait!" said Margo. She squinted and saw the end of the path just a few feet away. "I think we can make it if we jump."

"What do you mean jump? My feet are stuck to the ground like melted marshmallows!"

"Your *feet* aren't stuck," said Margo, bending down to untie her shoelace.

Shivers was shocked. "Margo, you'd better not be saying what I think you're saying."

"You have to leave your bunny slippers behind."

"No!" Shivers cried in a panic. "They aren't just my bunnies, they're my buddies!"

"It's the only way," Margo said. "Here, look."

She leaped right out of her shoes and cleared the path, landing on a pile of leaves.

Shivers shifted in his slippers. "If I take these off, I'll expose my toes and those horrible nails!" he wailed.

"Don't look down!" Margo said, shaking her head. She never thought she'd have to say that to him while he was standing on solid ground.

"Okay," Shivers said in a shaky voice. He began to slide his foot out of the slipper while looking straight up at the sky. But then he saw the crescent moon beaming above the trees and he screamed, "AAGH! A giant toenail!"

"Don't look up, either," Margo said, exasperated. "Just look straight ahead. And make it quick. Unless you want Quincy Thomas to slurp up your soul."

Hearing that was enough to make Shivers squirm right out of his slippers. He sprang into the air and came crashing down on the leaf pile like an oversize acorn.

He waved at his slippers. "Good-bye for now, bunny babies! I'll be back for you!"

Margo knew that the faster she covered up Shivers's feet, the less screaming she would have to hear. She searched through her big green backpack and found two brown paper lunch bags. She dumped out the food, then stuck Shivers's feet inside.

"Why did you pack two lunches this morning?" Shivers asked.

"I always pack two. Just in case you show up."
She shrugged.

Shivers and Margo marched through the dirt and leaves. Over the sound of the paper bags crinkling, they could hear the faint screams of more pirates behind them.

"My boots are stuck!" shouted a gruff voice.

"Being cursed is the worst!" bellowed another.

"What kind of sick ghost glues bunnies to the ground?" cried a third.

Shivers and Margo shuddered and shuffled on until they finally made it out of the trees.

There was a steep hill in front of them. Several pirates were climbing it with treasure in tow. When Shivers and Margo reached the base, they were faced with a truly terrible sight. . . . Faces! Floating on the hill with no bodies attached. It was too dark to see them clearly, but the outlines of their horrible heads were more than enough to make Shivers want to head home.

THE HiLL of HeadS
Home to the left over
heads from Quincy's
latest Pirate Feast!!

Margo saw a sign staked into the grass. "The Hill of Heads," she read. "Home to the leftover heads from Quincy's latest pirate feast."

"How about we stop reading things?" Shivers yelped.

"Okay," Margo agreed. "But you have to admit, this place is very well labeled."

"What are we going to do? What if the heads see us? What if they *touch* us?" Shivers fretted.

"Give me your coat," said Margo.

Shivers took off his velvet pirate coat. Margo draped it over them both so they could hide underneath. "Phew!" Margo said, plugging her nose. "This ghost must be close. It smells worse in here than Mrs. Beezle's breakfast breath does."

"I know." Shivers coughed. "This coat is a real stink sack. Let's get this over with!"

They rushed up the steep incline, crouching as low as they could. They shook with terror, knowing the horrible heads were hovering just above them. Even Albee was shivering. Or maybe he was just swimming; it was impossible to tell.

When they finally made it to the top of the hill, Margo whipped off the coat and handed it back to Shivers.

"AGGH! Another head!" Shivers screamed.

"It's just *my* head," said Margo.

"Oh. Did anyone ever tell you your head looks terrifying in the dark?" Shivers said, putting his coat back on.

Margo looked all around, but she could barely see anything in the dim moonlight.

"Where is this graveyard?" she wondered.

Then, as if in answer to her question, a torrent of terrified pirates rushed toward them with their arms in the air and surprise in the whites of their eyes. They were all shrieking so loudly that Margo was afraid her eardrums were going to explode.

When the pirates finally passed, Margo said, "This is the first time I've ever seen so many pirates who are just as scared as you are."

"I've been trying for years to tell everyone how scary the world is. I'm glad some people are finally starting to listen!" Shivers said. "Now let's bury this treasure and get out of here! I've got so many goosebumps, I'm afraid someone might mistake me for a goose!"

"I don't think that's how it works," said Margo.

"That's *definitely* not how it works," said Albee.

They shuffled along the path, trying not to trip in the darkness, until they reached the cemetery gate. Margo took a deep breath and opened it, the rusty metal wheezing like an old cat.

The haunted graveyard was more chilling than Shivers had ever imagined. There were rows and rows of gravestones dimly lit by the cool moonlight. It was overgrown with weeds that crept out of the ground and clutched onto the graves like spiders' legs. One tombstone towered above the rest. There was a single candle at its base, casting creepy shadows and lighting up the words carved into the marble: HERE LIES QUINCY THOMAS THE PIRATE. There were several freshly dug holes in the ground in front of it.

Margo squinted at her watch. "Shivers, you're almost out of time. It's now or never. And I mean *never.*" She gave him a firm shove toward the grave.

Shivers took a deep breath. Then, in the time it took for him to let out a single horrified scream-to-end-all-screams, he sprinted to the gravestone, burrowed into the dirt with his hands, reached into his pocket, threw the treasure into the hole, kicked a pile of dirt over it, then ran past Margo, through the gate, and all the way out of the graveyard.

Margo chased after him, screaming a little bit herself just to make sure she was following the instructions correctly. When she caught up to Shivers, she grabbed his hand and pumped it in the air like he was a champion.

"You did it, Shivers! You're uncursed!" she cheered.

"You're right!" Shivers stopped panting and started chanting. "Un-cursed! Un-cursed! Un-"

THUD!

Shivers tripped on a tree root and tumbled to the ground.

"Are you okay?!" Margo bent down to help him up.

"I think so," he said, rubbing his knees through torn pantaloons.

Just then, something caught Margo's eye—and it was the last thing she wanted to see: A diamond. Attached to a dog collar. On the ground.

"Shivers!" She picked up the collar. "You didn't bury the treasure!"

"What?!" He stared at the diamond in dismay. "Then what *did* I bury?!"

"I don't know, but you'd better fix this fast!"

Shivers leaped back up to his feet. They raced as fast as they could back to the graveyard. They flung open the cemetery gate, but they came to a dead stop when they saw a shadowy figure emerging from behind Quincy Thomas's gravestone. At that moment, Margo's watch began to beep.

Margo gripped Shivers's arm and whispered, "We're too late. It's midnight."

Shivers gulped. "Happy birthday to me."

CHAPTER ELEVEN

BOOM! A BRIGHT LIGHT blasted out from where the ghost stood, blinding Shivers, Margo, and Albee.

Shivers fell to his knees. "I see it! I see the light at the end of the tunnel! DEATH IS NEAR! Please, Quincy Thomas, just make it quick! And promise that there's lots of popcorn waiting for me on the other side! Albee, take care of my things! Margo, take care of Albee! And tell the people at the ice-cream shop I'm sorry I never paid my tab!"

"SHIVERS!" Margo snapped. "I can see the light, too."

Shivers's eyes popped like two corn kernels.

"HE'S GOING TO KILL US ALL!"

"Who are you?" shouted the figure behind the light.

"I'm Shivers the Pirate," he said, crawling through the dirt. "You've been following me all day and it's my birthday and I know that now you have to eat me. Just so you know, I'm mostly made of soft foods."

Margo was just as scared as Shivers was, but she wasn't going to give in without putting up a fight. She planted Albee's bottle firmly on the ground, gritted her teeth, balled up her fists, and charged. "Nobody eats my friends!" she shouted, running straight into the light. But before she got too far, she collided with something and came crashing down to the ground.

"Owie!" whined a high voice behind her. "Owie! Owie! Owie!"

It seemed like a very odd thing for a ghost to say. Margo sat up and saw the bright light on the ground just a few feet away. She scrambled over and realized that it was really just a flashlight. She picked it up and pointed it behind her. Standing in the pool of light was the strangest-looking person she had ever seen. He had the body of a small man but the head of a little baby. He had big blue eyes, curly blond hair, and a plump pink tongue that stuck just a tiny bit out of his mouth. The shovel in his hand and the dirt on his knees made it clear that he had just been digging up the treasure in front of the grave. He glared into the light and launched into a full-blown hissy fit.

"Get that light off me!" he cried. "What are you doing back here, anyway? What part of 'run away screaming and *never return*' don't you understand?!"

"Who are you?" Margo said in astonishment.

"Margo, it's the ghost of Quincy Thomas the Pirate! Can't you see?" Shivers turned to the man. "I'm sorry, Mr. Ghost, she's not a pirate. She doesn't understand how scary you are."

The man cleared his throat and in a much deeper voice than before he said, "That's right! I'm the ghost. BOO!"

"AAAGGH!" Shivers screamed.

The man continued, "Now get out of here! And never bury moldy string cheese at my grave again!" He held up a piece of green, rubbery cheese.

"*That's* what I buried?!" Shivers said. "But how did it get in my pocket?"

Margo sniffed the air around her and smelled a disgusting yet somehow familiar stench. Then, like the cheese from Shivers's pocket, she began to string things together. "That piece of cheese must have fallen in your pocket when we were on the trash barge. And that's what was causing the foul odor, not a ghost!"

The man sputtered, "It was! It was a ghost! I mean, it was me! BOO!"

"But Margo," Shivers said, "what about when I became merciless and violent? The string cheese didn't make me do that."

Margo was skeptical. "Shivers, when you threw that book, were you even aiming for Handsome's face?"

He thought back and admitted, "Actually, now that you mention it, I was trying to throw it at the floor to make a scary noise. I just have really bad aim."

Margo narrowed her eyes in suspicion. "I'm starting to think there was no curse in the first place."

"That's preposterous!" said the man, squirming in his boots.

Shivers was shocked. "No curse?! But what about this terrifying cape of ghostly horrors? I used to be really into capes, but today has just turned me off! I'm back to bibs and bibs only! I mean, when you think about it, a cape is just a big backward bib—"

"Shivers!" Margo interrupted. "I think it's time to shed some night-light on the Cape of Cods."

"NO!" said the man, grabbing Margo's arm.

She shook him off with ease and he tumbled to the ground. Then she turned the bright flashlight on the Hill of Heads. In the light, Shivers could see that the hill had no heads at all. "It's just a bunch of floating balloons with faces

The Hill of Heads
Home to the left over heads from Quincy's latest Pirate Feast!!

drawn on them!" he said, shaking his own head in disbelief.

Then Margo swung the light around to the Path of Lost Souls. They could see that it was paved with chewed-up gum.

"It's not the Path of Lost Souls, it's just a path of lost soles, because everyone loses their shoes when they get stuck in the gum!" Margo explained.

"What about the Bottomless Pit of Despair?" Shivers asked.

She shone the light as far as it would go. "Hm . . . that really is a bottomless pit. But I bet there aren't any bones in it!"

"So this is all fake?!" Shivers shouted. Then he turned back to the small man. "Then who's this guy?!"

"I told you: I'm the ghost of Quincy Thomas the Pirate! Can't you read?!" he said, stomping his feet and pointing at the tombstone behind him.

Margo looked back and forth between the man and the tombstone, and all at once, everything became perfectly clear. She took a permanent marker out of her big green backpack and began to cross out letters on the gravestone. When she was finally finished, she stepped aside and shone the light on her work.

"Here lies Q.T. Pi," she read aloud. Then she pointed the light directly in the man's face. "More like here *lies* Cutie Pie!"

Shivers froze in stupefied silence. He stared at the small man and realized that Margo was right. It was the same adorable face he had seen in the pirate book: Cutie Pie, the pirate zero.

Shivers opened his mouth. But instead of his usual "AAAAGH!" he let out an incredible "AWWWWWW!"

With that, Cutie Pie burst into tears. He flopped down on his stomach, kicking his feet and pounding his fists on the ground.

Shivers couldn't help but squeal at all the cuteness. "Look at those cute little kicks! He looks like a baby puppy trying to swim!"

Cutie Pie scowled, pulling himself to his feet. He took a giant lollipop out of his back pocket and slurped at it while fat tears streamed down his pink cheeks.

"Look!! He has a lollipop!!" Shivers gushed. He couldn't help it. Everything Cutie Pie did was irresistibly adorable. "AWWWW!"

"WAAAAH!" Cutie Pie cried. He threw the lollipop to the ground in frustration, then pointed a stubby plump finger at Shivers. "I'll get you for this, Shivers the Pirate!" he shrieked. "You'll regret the day you called me cute!" Then he ran from the graveyard and disappeared into a grove of tall pine trees.

Shivers smiled. "Even his threats are cute!" He grabbed Margo's hands and they jumped around in a joyous circle.

"I'm not cursed anymore!" shouted Shivers.

"You were never cursed to begin with!" Margo shouted back.

"Oh, yeah!"

They grabbed Albee and began to head back to the *Groundhog.*

"I can't believe that was Cutie Pie!" Margo marveled.

"I know. And all this talk about pie is making me want to go home and eat some!" said Shivers, patting his belly. "When you think about it, I mean *really* think about it, every pie is cute in its own way."

They strolled back through the graveyard gate and into the forest.

As they dodged the roots and rocks in the darkness, Albee stared up at the sky. He was the only one who saw the enormous flock of white parrots flying straight toward the other pirate ships.

"Uh-oh," said Albee.
But nobody heard him.

CHAPTER TWELVE

SHIVERS SKIPPED ALONG THE path, as joyous as Margo had ever seen him. He was babbling happily about his big birthday plans.

"Now that I'm actually getting to *celebrate* this birthday instead of being eaten by a ghost, I think I want to go all out. I'm going to take a bath with all of my rubber duckies. *All* of them! Plus, I have so much singing and sleeping to do. I'm going to nap, I'm going to clap, and when I hit that dance deck, I'm going to tap!" His eyes grew wide with excitement. "And you know what I've always wanted to do? Eat a whole ham!"

Margo laughed and tried to keep up with

Shivers. After all, she was the one holding the flashlight, and she didn't want him to crack his skull on the Hill of Heads.

"What should I get you for your birthday?" Margo asked.

"You don't have to get me anything. Your presence is my present." Shivers gasped. "Hey, I bet that's the first time anyone has ever said that! I should add it to my notebook of original quotations. Which reminds me, can you get me a notebook for my birthday? And a pencil? But not the sharp kind. I want a big, dull pencil!"

They reached the top of the Hill of Heads and Shivers smiled. "This place is actually pretty great now that I know all these heads are really balloons. It's like a party up here!" He started poking the balloons, sending them higher up into the air. "Wow, Cutie Pie did a great job on this one!" he said, stopping in front of one of the balloons. "It looks so lifelike! It even has a whole body attached! But I wonder why he decided to make it so ugly. . . ." He jabbed at it with his finger.

"OW!"

"AAAAGH!" Shivers screamed.

Margo pointed the flashlight at the balloon, which wasn't a balloon at all, but a hideous head. "FOOTSOME!" she shouted.

"And did anyone notice this extremely handsome balloon?" said Handsome Ransom, stepping into the light and smiling a dazzling smile.

Shivers, Margo, and Albee all took a step back.

"The parrots came to us with a new message from Quincy Thomas. . . ." Footsome sneered.

Then he put his fingers up to his pale, cracked lips and let out a shrill whistle. With that, a stampede of pirates crested the Hill of Heads, snarling and scowling.

Shivers and Margo looked at each other nervously out of the corners of their eyes.

"What was the message?" Shivers squeaked.

Footsome grinned and pointed right at him. "'Bring me the head of Shivers the Pirate!'"

All at once, there was a loud SHINK! as the pirates drew their swords and moved in closer.

As the light cast over their ferocious, grizzled faces, Shivers could see the desperation in their eyes. He tried to say something, but his speech turned into a stutter, which sputtered into a mutter, and the words were just too afraid to come out.

Margo stepped forward. "You don't have to do this! Ghosts aren't real!"

"Of course ghosts are real!" said a pudgy pirate with a mud-caked face. "What else could be haunting me from beyond the grave? I smell terrible!"

A pirate with a rusty hook for a hand stepped forward. "And I'm mercilessly violent! It's definitely because of a ghost! Now come here so I can cut off your head!"

Shivers shrieked as he and Margo took another step back.

"You're certain that ghosts are real?" Margo said.

"Yes!" said the entire group all at once.

"And they're terrifying!" said a voice from the back.

"Well, then, you must be right," she said, putting her hand on her hip. "Ghosts *are* real." She flicked off the flashlight, plunging the Hill of Heads into total terrifying darkness. Then she shouted at the top of her lungs, "BOO!"

For the first time in his life, Shivers was the only pirate who didn't scream.

"AAAAGH!" the pirates shrieked at the night

sky. They scattered in different directions, crashing into one another. The sounds of swords clanging with belt buckles and bootstraps tangling up in pirate hats rang into the night as Margo grabbed Shivers's sleeve and made a run for it.

"Are we going back to the *Groundhog*?" Shivers wheezed as he struggled to keep up.

Margo shook her head. "No. They'll be waiting for us there. We're going to find Cutie Pie and show everybody what a big phony he is. It's the only way to stop that mob and keep your head exactly where it belongs."

"On a pillow?"

"On your shoulders," Margo said, leading Shivers into the grove of pine trees where Cutie Pie had fled.

As they made their way through the forest, the sounds of pirate bellows and popping balloons grew fainter, but the tree branches grew thicker, tickling their shoulders and casting eerie shadows in the milky moonlight.

"Could you please turn the flashlight back on?" Shivers asked.

"It's too dangerous. I don't want them to find us," Margo explained.

Luckily for Shivers, a flicker of light appeared just a little way ahead. They took a few steps forward and saw that the soft glow was coming from the windows of a big stone cottage that sat in a clearing just beyond the trees. A plume of smoke puffed up out of a chimney on the roof. Chubby lawn gnomes made of stone sat next to the

front step with friendly smiles on their faces. The entire cottage looked welcoming and inviting, but the front yard was covered in signs that said YOU'RE *NOT* WELCOME and NO ONE INVITED YOU!

Margo ignored the signs and tiptoed up to the side of the house.

"Margo, wait! The sign says no one invited us!"

"No one ever invites us, Shivers. Now, come on!"

Shivers squirmed his way up next to her and they peered through a window into the cottage.

The first thing they saw inside was a packed treasure chest as big as a bathtub. There was so much gold spilling out, it looked like an overstuffed grilled cheese sandwich.

"I think we're in the right place," Margo whispered.

As they looked more closely around the cottage, they began to notice that it looked like a baby's nursery. The room was painted bright blue, unicorn posters covered the walls, and there was a giant crib in the corner. Then they heard a creaking noise coming from the other side of the room. They smushed their faces up to the window and gasped. There was Cutie Pie, wearing footie pajamas, holding a sippy cup, and riding furiously on a rocking horse. It was truly one of the most adorable things either of them had ever seen. Shivers tried to contain himself, but emotions spilled out of him like a rushing river bursting through a beaver dam. He couldn't help but let out a spectacular "AAAAWWW!"

Before Margo could quiet Shivers down, a pair of pirates seized them, turning Shivers's happy "AAAWWW" into an ear-piercing

"AAAA AAGGGHHH!!!"

CHAPTER THIRTEEN

AS THE PIRATES DRAGGED Shivers, Margo, and Albee away from the window, Shivers pleaded, "AAAGH! Please don't chop off my head! I need it! For screaming! AAAAAGHH!"

One of the pirates wore a pointy hat with an arrow sticking out of the top. He had crossed eyes and a flat nose that looked like it had been squished into his face. The other wore thick rubber gloves and steel-toed boots that clanked when he walked. The cross-eyed pirate reached out his hand. Shivers was sure he was about to pop off his noggin but instead, he opened the door to the cottage. The pirates hauled Shivers and Margo inside and tossed them into the giant crib. Then they swung a set of wooden bars over the top. The cross-eyed pirate secured the bars with a huge metal lock and put the key in his pocket.

Albee shook his head, Margo shook the bars of the crib, and Shivers just shook all over. They were trapped.

Cutie Pie climbed down from his rocking horse and took a long, slow drink from his sippy cup. Then he threw the cup to the ground, where it made no mess at all.

"Well, well, well," he said, pitter-pattering over in his soft pajama footies. "If it isn't Mr. Clever and Miss Smarty-Pants and . . . a fish."

"That's Mr. Fish to you," said Albee.

"I don't know how you managed to escape the pirate mob, but it doesn't matter now. My crew and I will take care of you ourselves and make sure that the world never hears another peep from Shivers the Pirate."

Cutie Pie and his crew of two giggled menacingly.

Shivers turned to Margo and cried, "They're going to chop off my head!" He looked around the crib. "What a waste. There are so many comfy pillows in here!"

"Chop off your head?" Cutie Pie made a face like he had just sucked on a lemon. "Ewie ewie ewie! That's gross! I'm not going to chop off your head. Do you know how messy that would be? I'm going to keep you locked in here until you're nothing but a rotting pile of bones."

"You're going to leave us in here to starve?" Margo said, her ears turning red with rage.

"Precisely!" said Cutie Pie. He held out his hand and the cross-eyed pirate gave him the key to the padlock. Then, he marched over to a helium tank next to the crib. "This is where we make the 'heads' for our Hill of Heads." He chuckled. He blew up a big red balloon and knotted it around the key. "We won't be needing this for a long, long time." He let the balloon go and it floated up toward the high stone ceiling, taking the key with it.

Margo and Shivers noticed there were several household items attached to balloons on the ceiling.

"I keep lots of things I don't use up there. It's a great space saver!" Cutie Pie said as the key came to a stop right next to a pair of running shoes and a pack of floss. "By the time that key comes down, you'll be the stars of the newest attraction on my haunted cape . . . The Cage of Rib Cages!"

Shivers screamed and tried to hide under the crib covers.

"Ah, the sound of screams is like music to my ears." Cutie Pie picked up a pie that was cooling on the windowsill, then plunged his plump little fingers into it, scooping out a slice and shoveling it into his mouth. "And I'll make many more pirates scream for years to come with the help of your rattling bones, Shivers the Pirate!"

"Bring me the head of Shivers the Pirate!" squawked a white parrot. There was a whole pack of them sitting in a cage near the fireplace.

Cutie Pie glanced at the parrots and smirked. "They're so well trained. They'll say anything I want if I repeat it enough. Then all I have to do is cover them in parrot-safe white paint and every stupid pirate thinks they're ghost parrots from the grave of Quincy Thomas! Hee-hee!" He laughed an adorably evil laugh.

"But why?" Shivers asked. "Why did you create this terrible, terrifying trick? What did pirates ever do to you?"

"They laughed at me! They laughed at all of us!" Cutie Pie shouted. He put the pie down on a table, then pointed at the cross-eyed pirate. "They laughed at Captain Whichway here because he has no sense of direction. Watch this. Whichway, which way is West?"

Whichway pointed East.

"Which way is North?"

Whichway pointed up.

"See?" Cutie Pie said. Then he pointed at the pirate wearing rubber gloves. "And this walking disaster is Butterfingers. Everyone laughed at him because he's the clumsiest pirate to ever crash into the sea. He's dropped so many swords, he has to wear steel-toed boots to keep from slicing his feet off."

At that moment, there was a loud CRASH! behind them. Butterfingers had tried to get a piece of pie but he ended up dropping the whole thing on the floor. He looked up bashfully.

"Look at the mess you've made, Butterfingers!" Cutie Pie scolded. "Whichway, get the broom from the closet and clean this up."

"You've got it, boss!" said Whichway, then he walked out the front door.

"WAAH!" Cutie Pie cried, balling up his fists and stomping his little footies on the ground. "Butterfingers, go find him!"

"Yes, sir!" Butterfingers fumbled his way out the door.

Shivers was beginning to understand. "And they must have laughed at you because you're so cute."

Cutie Pie whirled around with daggers in his eyes. They were cute daggers–really more like toothpicks. "I'm *not* cute! I scare pirates! I steal all their treasure! And I live in a terrifying fortress!"

Margo was more confused than a T-shirt in a tuxedo shop. "Terrifying fortress? You have unicorn posters all over your walls!"

"That's right! What's more terrifying than horses with spears coming out of their heads?!"

"He has a point," muttered Shivers.

"But you sleep in a giant crib!" Margo said, rattling the bars in front of her.

"It's not a crib!" Cutie Pie insisted, sticking his tongue out at her. "It's a high-security bed."

"But why do you have bars on the *top*?" Margo asked.

"To prevent aerial attacks!" Cutie Pie said, angrily twisting the tiny blond curls on top of his head.

Margo looked Cutie Pie in his cutie eye. "If you don't want people to say you're cute, maybe you shouldn't wear footie pajamas and drink from a sippy cup."

"MY FEET GET COLD AND I'M ALWAYS ON THE GO!" Cutie Pie shouted at the top of his tiny lungs.

Shivers could see what was about to happen but he couldn't stop it. Margo's forehead crinkled and her eyes grew wide and she busted out into laughter so loud she almost cracked in half.

"Stop it! Stop making that horrible noise!" He walked right up to the crib so that his little button nose pushed in between the bars. "I hate laughter! My whole life, pirates have laughed at me. So I made up a little ghost story to scare the pantaloons off of them. And they all fell for it! Now I've got more treasure than any pirate in the Seven Seas!"

He grabbed two handfuls of gold coins from his overflowing treasure chest and tossed them in the air. They clattered to the floor, rolling in all different directions. Some even got stuck in the sticky pie mush.

Shivers had to admit that Cutie Pie had come up with quite a master plan. But there were still some things he couldn't figure out. "How did you know a drop of water would hit the deck of my new ship?"

"Pirate ships are in the middle of the ocean! Of course they're going to get wet!" Cutie Pie giggled.

"But what about the curse signs? How did you know that a foul odor would follow me?" Shivers asked.

"A foul odor follows every pirate! We all stink like fish!" said Cutie Pie.

Albee was outraged.

"How did you know I would become merciless and violent?" Shivers asked.

"All pirates are merciless and violent! It's our thing!" Cutie Pie explained. "It was the perfect trick. I got my revenge. And it's as sweet as this giant piece of bubble gum!" He unwrapped some pink bubble gum and popped it into his mouth. "Mmm . . . yummy yummy yummy yummy yummy!"

"Yummy yummy!" the parrots repeated.

The front door swung open and Butterfingers came stomping through, holding up Whichway's pointy hat. "I found him!" he said triumphantly.

"That's just his hat!" Cutie Pie screeched.

"Oh, I must have dropped the rest of him." Butterfingers sighed.

At that moment, Whichway came crashing through the window face-first. "I'm back!" he announced. And at *that* moment, Shivers realized why Whichway had such a flat nose.

"You guys! You totally interrupted the end of my revenge speech!" Cutie Pie whined, stomping around in his footies like a baby elephant having a bad day.

"Sorry!" said Whichway. "Hey, since when does the door have so much glass in it?"

Cutie Pie smacked his forehead. Then he turned back to Shivers. "Well, you know what they say. You don't pick your crew, your crew picks you. They said we were all pirate zeroes. But look at us now!"

"You think you're pirate heroes?!" Margo said incredulously.

"We're even better than that. We're pirate FEAR-Os!" Cutie Pie tried to high-five his crew, but Butterfingers missed and fell into the floor pie, and Whichway ended up high-fiving the rocking horse.

Shivers decided it was time to take a stand. But when he tried, he hit his head on the crib bars. So he decided it was time to take a sit, while still saying something he believed in.

"Scaring people is wrong!" he shouted.

"It's right!" Cutie Pie snarled.

"It's left!" cried Whichway.

"You don't understand!" Shivers continued. "Do you know how horrifying it is to be scared all the time?! Do you know how scarifying it is to be horrified all the time?! It's terrifying! Life is frightening enough already without you making up ghost stories! I mean, have you ever really *looked* at a toaster? Have you ever *studied* a toenail? Have you ever closed your eyes and realized just how dark the world can be without a night-light? And it's even darker because of Big Baby Bullies like you!"

"Oh, I'm a Big Baby Bully?" Cutie Pie scoffed as he chewed away at his bubble gum. "Well, you, Shivers the Pirate, are the biggest zero there is. Soon there will be nothing left of either of you, and no one will ever know that Quincy Thomas the Pirate was just a big trick." He looked

Shivers straight in the eye and began to blow a bubble with his gum. The pink bubble grew and grew until it was the size of Cutie's adorable baby head, and then it exploded with a POP!

And with that POP!, Shivers and Margo remembered the bubble gum bubble that Albee blew on the trash barge that afternoon. And they got an idea. Shivers looked down at Albee in his bottle. Margo looked up at the parrots in the cage. Then they looked at each other and nodded.

"Excuse me, Mr. Pie?" said Margo, plastering a confused look on her face. "I don't understand. Quincy Thomas the Pirate isn't real?"

"Weren't you listening? Pirate ghosts aren't real! It was all a big trick!" Cutie Pie said proudly.

"What did you say?" Margo asked, holding her hand up to her ear like she couldn't hear.

"I said pirate ghosts aren't real! It was all a big trick!" Cutie repeated, more loudly this time.

"I still can't hear you! I must have seawater in my ear!" Margo said with an exaggerated shrug.

"PIRATE GHOSTS AREN'T REAL! PIRATE GHOSTS AREN'T REAL! PIRATE GHOSTS AREN'T REAL! IT WAS ALL A BIG TRICK!" Cutie Pie shouted over and over again, jumping up and down.

Then there was a soft squawking from the parrot cages. At first, it was just one bird saying, "Pirate ghosts aren't real! It was all a big trick!"

Then one by one, the others joined in until the whole flock was screeching, "PIRATE GHOSTS AREN'T REAL! IT WAS ALL A BIG TRICK!"

Cutie Pie scowled at the birds. "Stop it! Stop saying that!"

But their squawks were so loud now that they couldn't even hear him.

"Now, Shivers!" said Margo.

Shivers popped the top off of Albee's bottle. "You ready, buddy?"

"I was born ready," Albee said.

Shivers poured Albee into his hand, thrust him through the bars of the crib, and attached him to the nozzle of the helium machine faster than Cutie Pie could say "WAH!"

Albee blew up to his full blowfish size, just like he had on the trash barge. But this time, he was filled with floaty helium that lifted him straight to the ceiling, where the key to the crib was still suspended on a balloon string. Albee reached out a spiky fin and popped the balloon.

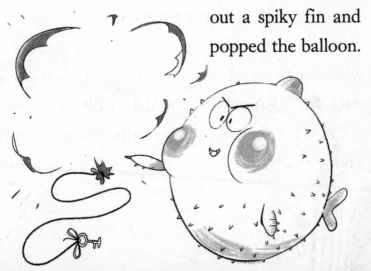

The key fell straight down and into Margo's hand. She opened the lock and pushed away the bars above her. Then she and Shivers leaped out of the crib like two really big bouncing babies.

"Grab them!" Cutie Pie wailed.

Butterfingers lunged at Margo, but she spun around, sending him careening into the wall, where he ended up plastered against a picture of a unicorn.

All the spinning and screaming and squawking had Whichway so mixed up he didn't know which "them" to grab, so he just grabbed Cutie Pie and squeezed tightly. "Got 'em!" he said.

Cutie Pie tried to shake Whichway off of him, but then he froze in horror when he saw Shivers standing next to the parrot cage.

"You wouldn't dare. You're a coward! You're a nobody! You're a zero!"

"No, I'm not!" said Shivers. He remembered what Margo had said, that only he could make himself a hero. And that's exactly what he did.

He wrapped his fingers around the door of the birdcage and flung it open. The entire flock of parrots flooded the room, squawking, "PIRATE GHOSTS AREN'T REAL! IT WAS ALL A BIG TRICK!" They flapped their white wings all the way out the broken window, carrying their message out to the cape.

"WAAAAH!" Cutie Pie bellowed.

Knowing his work was done, Albee blew the helium out in one big breath. He let out a high-pitched "HEEEEE" as he deflated and drifted to the ground, where Shivers caught him and dropped him safely back into his bottle.

Cutie Pie's nostrils flared with rage. His head turned pink so it matched his plump little tongue. An angry vein bulged from his forehead as he let out a furious scream.

"KILL THEM!"

CHAPTER FOURTEEN

SHIVERS, MARGO, AND ALBEE bolted out of the cottage and headed straight for the beach. Cutie Pie and Whichway chased after them–Butterfingers tried, but he tripped over the lawn gnomes and had to give up. Shivers and Margo ran through the forest, darting around the branches. Soon the forest got so dense with trees that it was almost impossible to figure out where to go. They could hear Whichway and Cutie Pie's footsteps getting closer.

"Where do we go?" asked Shivers.

"NORTH!" Margo shouted, loud enough so she knew Whichway would hear her.

"Aha!" said Whichway, and he climbed straight to the top of a pine tree. Now only Cutie Pie was left chasing them.

Margo led Shivers and Albee along the edge of the forest, hoping that they would soon see something familiar. Finally she spotted the Hill of Heads. They sprinted for it as fast as they could. When they reached the edge, they saw Handsome and Footsome climbing up. They were leading a pack of haggard-looking pirates.

"Shivers the Pirate!" Handsome shouted. "We've been looking all over for you!"

Shivers and Margo came to a screeching halt.

"Oh no!" Shivers said nervously. "They didn't get the message!"

Footsome marched right up to Shivers, his flaky, cracked teeth edging into a smile.

Shivers gripped Albee's bottle and braced himself for the worst. With Cutie Pie behind him and Footsome in front of him, there was nowhere to run.

Footsome reached into the pocket of his dirt-crusted coat. Then, to everyone's surprise, he pulled out the diamond-studded dog collar. "You dropped this," he grunted.

Shivers shed the dread from his face and smacked on a big old smile. "So you're not going to chop off my head?"

"No!" said Handsome, sidling up next to Footsome. "Didn't you hear the great news? Pirate ghosts aren't real! It was all a big trick! Thank goodness those brilliant parrots figured that out."

Shivers and Albee gave each other a knowing glance.

"Sorry about the whole chopping-off-your-head thing," said Handsome.

"Yes," Footsome agreed. "People do crazy things when they think they're going to get eaten by a ghost."

Handsome shook Shivers's hand. Footsome shook Shivers's foot. It was odd.

"Now all we have to do is find the son of a sewer rat who tricked us and get our treasure back!" growled Footsome.

"I think we can help you with that," said Margo.

Just then, the sun peeked over the horizon, zipping a bright morning light across the Cape of Cods. Everyone began to hear the huffing and puffing of little baby lungs and the pitter-patter of pajamaed feet reaching the top of the hill.

"Meet the real ghost of Quincy Thomas the Pirate," said Shivers as Cutie Pie stepped into view.

The sunlight sparkled on his bouncy blond curls. His cheeks were rosy red from running and ranting. And a spot of morning dew dotted the tip of his button nose.

Cutie's eyes grew wide at the sight of the pirate

horde. He looked around nervously, not know-ing what to do or where to run. So he decided to scare them one last time. "Boo!"

This set off the loudest explosion of pirate laughter in the history of the world. They howled and whooped. They snickered and snorted. They cackled until their ribs crackled. All the while pointing right at Cutie.

"Stop it!" Cutie demanded, throwing his fists in the air and stomping around. "Stop laughing or I'll chop off all of your heads!"

This just made the pirates laugh even harder. They howled with hilarity. They giggled so hard,

they were doubled over with delight—one guy was even tripled over. Tears of laughter spilled from their eyes and pooled into puddles on the ground.

Cutie Pie jammed his plump little fingers into his ears to try to silence the laughter. But if there's one thing everyone knows about pirates (besides the fact that they smell bad and are mercilessly violent), it's that they're really, really loud. There was no escaping the sound.

"Well, Cutie Pie, I guess your jig is up," said Shivers. "But my jig has just begun!" He launched into a happy little tap dance.

Cutie Pie's face turned as purple as a grape-flavored Popsicle.

"Your head is mine, Shivers the Pirate!"

He reached into his pocket and pulled out a silver dagger. Or maybe it was an adorable little sword. Either way, it was very, very sharp. He held it above his head and charged straight at Shivers.

Shivers screamed a scream he was sure would be his last.

The dagger was just inches away from dividing Shivers in two when, suddenly, Cutie Pie's feet slid on the puddle of pirate tears. In the same slippery way that Quincy Thomas had met his demise, Cutie fell over the edge of the Hill of Heads.

He flapped his arms wildly like a chicken trying to fly, but it was too late. He tumbled down the hill, bounced past the Path of Lost Souls, and finally fell straight into the Bottomless Pit of Despair.

For a moment, everything was quiet. Then there was a soft thud.

"I guess it's not bottomless after all," said Shivers.

The throng of pirates burst into happy cheers.

"He's gone!" said one of the pirates.

"We'll never be tricked by a ghost again!" said another.

"AAAGH! Who said ghost?!" said a third.

Shivers and Margo pointed the pirates toward the cottage, where they could find Cutie Pie's collection of stolen treasure—and his rocking horse, if anyone wanted it. The pirates all took off down the hill, clinking and clanking their swords with excitement.

Handsome and Footsome lingered behind.

"Thank you, Shivers the Pirate," said Handsome, the morning sun bouncing off his perfectly chiseled cheek dimples. "Are you coming to get your share of the treasure?"

"The only thing I need is my bunny slippers," Shivers said, looking at the tattered lunch bags on his feet. "They're still stuck on the path."

"All of our shoes are stuck on the path. That cute little pirate was trying to steal our treasure *and* our footwear," said Footsome, spit spraying from his mouth. "Though I suppose it's nice for my toes to get some fresh air."

Without thinking, Shivers looked down at

Footsome's bare feet. And he saw something very strange. There were no nails. With a combination of curiosity and caution he asked, "Where are your toenails?"

Footsome smiled and tapped the gnarled set of teeth in his mouth. "Right here!"

"AAAAAAGGGGHHH!"

☠ ☠ ☠

When they got back to the *Groundhog*, Margo set sail for New Jersey Beach and Shivers announced that he was seven naps behind schedule. He wrapped himself in his marshmallow comforter and promptly fell asleep, his feet tucked snugly into his bunny slippers. He dreamed of s'mores and snored the whole way home.

Margo stood at the helm, the morning waves whisking sea salt onto her ponytail. Albee was in his bottle next to her, swimming around and supervising. It made Margo wonder: *Do fish ever sleep? And if so, is it on a water bed?*

It wasn't long before Shivers woke up to the familiar sounds of waves lapping against the sandy shore and kids complaining as they stood in a long line for ice cream. He was home. He sat up smiling. It was his birthday. He hadn't been eaten by a ghost. And there was a whole ham waiting for him in the fridge.

Suddenly, his bedroom door burst open.

"SURPRISE!"

"AAAAGH!" Shivers shouted, diving for cover under the covers.

"I told you that was a bad idea," said Bob.

His parents, Brock, Margo, and Albee crowded into his bedroom. They were throwing pirate confetti (which was really just sand) and singing "Happy Birthday" (which was really just shouting).

"Come see your present, baby brother!" said Brock.

Brock yanked Shivers out of bed, hoisted him over his head, and hauled him down the hall, through the kitchen, and out onto the dance deck. Which was now officially a song and dance deck, because of the magnificent grand piano parked in the middle of it.

"My piano!" Shivers shouted, his eyes shining with excitement. He did a little dance over to it, then struck a chord on the keys. "Hey, this thing feels familiar!"

"We plundered it from a yacht!" said Tilda.

"But they seemed happy to get rid of it," said Bob. "They said something about 'grubby little kid hands' touching it."

Shivers stretched out his arms and smashed all the keys at once. "It's perfect." He sighed.

Margo tapped him on the shoulder. "I got you something, too."

She handed him a package wrapped entirely in empty chip bags. "It's the only wrapping paper I had. Plus, I got super hungry on the trip back."

Shivers immediately tore it open and was puzzled to see *The Pirate Book You've Been Looking For.* His forehead crinkled with worry. "Don't tell me I'm cursed again!"

"Nope!" Margo said.

She opened the book to the section on Pirate Heroes. There, on the very first page, was Shivers.

She looked at him with a big smile. "I thought, if this is a book of pirate history, then it had better be true."

THE END!

The story continues with

SHIVERS'S

next adventure.

Take a sneak peek!

CHAPTER ONE

SNAP!

Shivers the Pirate secured the goggles to his head. The downpour had already begun. He zipped up his wetsuit so his entire body was covered. Then he put on a pair of bright yellow dishwashing gloves and wrapped rubber bands around his wrists so not a single water droplet would seep in.

"In an emergency like this, it's always good to have extra protection on hand . . . and on foot!" he declared. He swapped out his usual bunny slippers for a pair of bunny flippers. As he took a squeaky step forward, fear rattled him like a tambourine. He knew what he had to do, but he really wished he had to *don't*.

Shivers's first mate, Albee, was supervising in his fishbowl just a few feet away. Albee knew that this could only end in disaster, but as a fish, there's only so much you can do. His only hope was that Shivers didn't try to use him as a flotation device.

Shivers turned to Albee and grimaced. "If I don't make it, just remember this: your fish flakes are in the cabinet. Don't eat too many at once. And never leave the stove on. In fact, don't even go near the stove." He stared straight into Albee's big fishy eyeballs. "Use the microwave instead!"

Shivers grabbed his snorkel, crammed it into his mouth, and leaped across the great divide. Sheets of rain pelted his goggles, blurring his sight. His sopping wet hair matted to his face. The rush of water was so strong it even seeped through his bunny flippers and tickled his toes. This was going worse than expected.

The water slapped violently against the ground. He stuck his fingers in his ears to protect against the sound, but also to make sure the water didn't wiggle its way into his head–Shivers had always been deathly afraid of getting brainwashed.

Heavy droplets battered his scrawny legs until he was weak in the knees. Pressure swelled inside of him like a balloon, until the only thing he could do was burst. He spat out the snorkel and screamed.

"AAAAAAAAAGHHH!"

But as soon as the scream started, it was snuffed out by a wave of water that funneled through Shivers's wide-open mouth. He coughed and stumbled, his flippers slipping underneath him. Shivers came crashing down with a splash as the rain pelted him harder than ever before.

"I'm drowning!" he wailed, thrashing left and splashing right.

"Pull yourself together!" Albee said, shaking his head–but because he's a fish, he was really shaking his whole body.

Then, through the misty rain, Shivers spotted his only hope for survival. He flipped onto his belly and stretched out his arm until his fingers touched a cold, metal lever. With his last ounce of strength, he gripped it as tightly as he could and pulled.

The water stopped.

Shivers hoisted himself out of the bathtub and bellowed, "I HATE TAKING SHOWERS!"

He threw on a fresh pair of pantaloons, his velvet pirate coat, and his feathered pirate cap. He stuffed his feet into his bunny slippers and picked up Albee's fishbowl. He stumbled down the hallway and collapsed on the kitchen floor in a heap.

"That was worse than I could have *ever* imagined," he cried.

"Well, you sure smell a whole lot better!" Standing above Shivers was his best friend, Margo Clomps'n'Stomps. She stared down at him with her big green eyes, her hands on her hips. As usual, she had a backpack on her back, a ponytail on her head, and a smile as wide as a mile.

"Why did you make me do that?" Shivers groaned.

"Shivers, yesterday for your birthday you ate six gallons of ice cream and a whole ham! You were covered in so much sugar and ham juice you smelled like a pig dipped in a Pixie Stix!"

Shivers sighed. Margo had a point. Sleeping in ham juice had been unpleasant. He dragged himself up from the floor and narrowed his eyes at her. "Fine. But I'm never taking a shower again!"

Margo laughed and shook her head.

Shivers opened his refrigerator. Now that the worst part of the day was surely over, he could eat some breakfast in peace. He mixed a banana and some pudding together in a big bowl. Banana pudding was his favorite new food. It was so soft, he almost wanted to lay his head down in it and fall asleep—but then he'd have to take another shower. So instead, he plunged in his spoon and took a bite.

"Mmm . . . mushy," he grinned.

Margo sat down at the table across from him. That's when he saw the crackling flame of adventure flare in her eyes. "Oh, no." Shivers waggled his finger. "I know what you're thinking, and it's got my stomach sinking. I'm going to tell you the same thing I told my family: I'm not going on any adventures today!"

Margo looked out the porthole and noticed that Shivers's parents' ship, *The Plunderer*, wasn't bobbing out at sea as usual. "Where did your family go?"

"Beats me! They left on a pirate mission early this morning. They said it was guaranteed to make me seasick, so I politely declined. Actually, I screamed and hid under my covers. I'm sure they'll be back by sunset as usual, and until then, I'm staying right here."

"Come on, Shivers!" Margo slapped her palms on the table. "You can't just sit there eating pudding all day!"

"Wanna bet?" Shivers said, cramming another spoonful in his mouth.

Margo pointed out the porthole at the open ocean. "But there's a whole world of excitement out there just waiting for us!"

"Maybe it's waiting for someone else," Shivers tried. "Hey, I've got an idea—let's play hide-and-seek! You go seek out adventure, and I'll hide here under this table. Just make sure to be back by sunset. I need someone to help me turn on my night-lights."

"But we're on a pirate ship! Let's set sail! Hit the high seas!" Margo was always itching for an exciting quest.

Shivers held up his hand. "First of all, I never hit anything. What if it hits back? Secondly, this pirate ship is designed specifically not to go on adventures. It's supposed to be safe, secure, and most importantly, extremely cozy. It's called the *Groundhog*, remember? And that's where it's going to stay: on the *ground*. Right here in the middle of New Jersey Beach, the safest place in the entire–AAAAAGGHHHH!!!"

At that moment, a heavy metal hook smashed through the porthole and landed on Shivers's kitchen floor. It was attached to a thick, mossy rope.

"MARGO!" Shivers screamed, leaping under the table. "What's going on?!"

"Only one way to find out," she said, grabbing his hand.

They ran outside to the deck and saw something so terrifying that even the pudding in Shivers's belly panicked.

Also by
ANNABETH BONDOR-STONE
and
CONNOR WHITE!

SHIVERS!

HARPER
An Imprint of HarperCollinsPublishers

www.harpercollinschildrens.co